WAR MISTRESS

JORDYN ALEXANDER

BOOK TWO
OF THE WAR BRIDES OF ADRIK

©2024

To my best friend, Valerie. You've always been a major support to me. Here's to many more years of friendship.

CONTENTS

FOREWORD

Hello lovely readers!

Here we are again at the beginning of a new book. I hope this finds you well and that you are relaxing with some well-deserved downtime, ready to devour a new book.

As always, I have some warnings for those who are maybe a little more sensitive and need some heads up about what they are getting into. For those that don't need them, skip right ahead and get straight to the book.

For those that *do* need them, there's no shame in your game. I, myself, like to check for warnings. For this book, they are:

Trigger Warnings:
Mentions of:
Past Non-Con Sex
Past Suicidal Ideation

Depictions of:
Torture
Violent Death
Forced Kissing (not by the MMC)
Near Incident of Non-Con Sex Act (not by the MMC)

If you are good to go, head on into the book. I'm excited for you! For those that need to put this down and look for lighter fare, I understand, and happy hunting.

Again, as always, my editor and I are only human. We can't possibly catch all of my mistakes. If you find an error please contact me with it at authorjordynalexander@gmail.com and win my undying gratitude. That way future editions can be more mistake-proof.

With all that out of the way, it's time. On with the show!

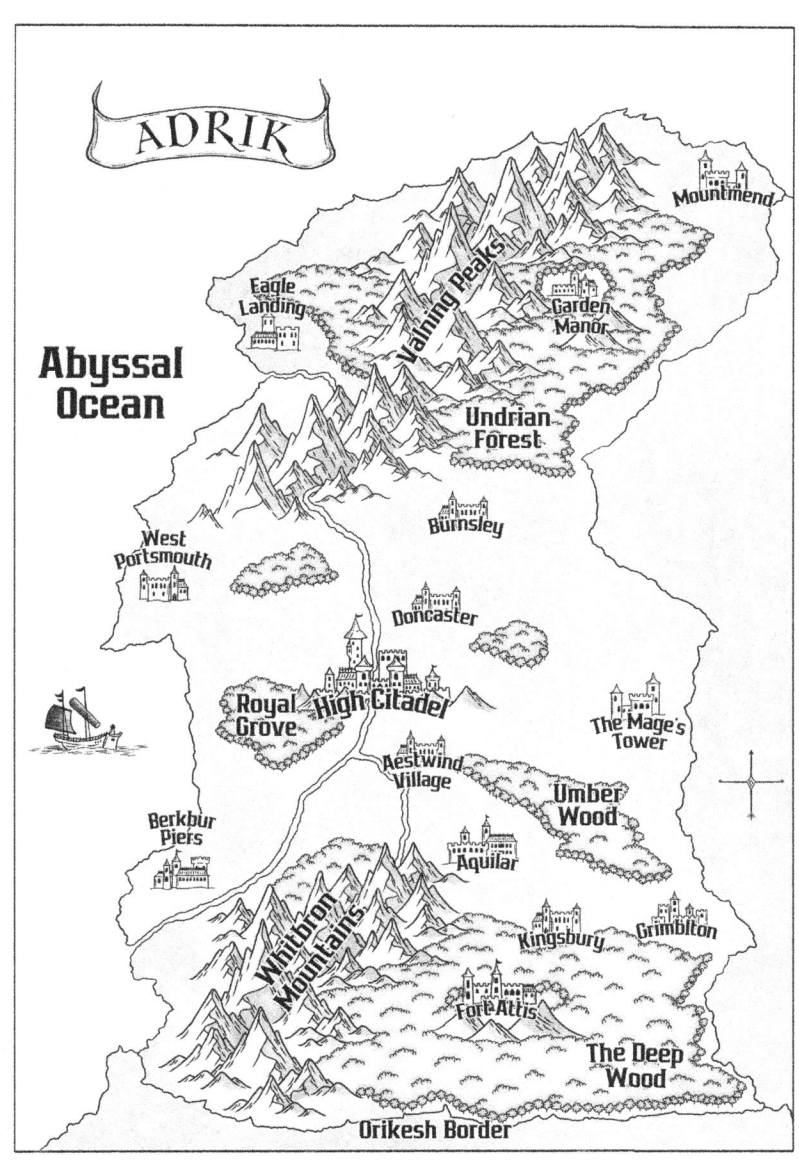

CHAPTER 1

Pellia

It was a mistake to agree to be the regent. The thought comes to me unbidden. Though it is true that I agreed to the task to help a friend, as I sit through my fifth mind-numbing meeting of the day I can't help but think, *Is this all ruling is?*

I suppose I can't say that I am ruling in truth. It is more about stewarding the nation while its true rulers reside in another kingdom, but so far that stewarding seems to be listening to a lot of bickering by nobles I can barely stand. One of them says, "—and if the Kimbers would pay a more fair share of the tribute then mayhap then we could pay more towards the rebuilding effort, but—"

"You offend my honor, sir!" snaps Duchess Kimber, dressed as usual in men's garments. "The Kimber lands took in more refugees from the south than any other province! We are paying what we can toward the tribute, while not unduly taxing the people. Winter is coming and—"

And blah, blah, blah, I say internally. I know that we need to be concerned about the people and how they will be able to make it through the winter, but I also know that Stella Kimber has never been concerned about the people or if they are unduly taxed in her life. She, just like everyone else in this room, is concerned with power, the gaining and keeping of it.

Except me. I couldn't care less about the intrigue and the in-fighting. I am adept in their ways. I can navigate it with my eyes closed, I have since I was a child and first met the now-dead king Yorian. In order to stay alive I had to agree to everything he said and never step on any toes. I learned to smile and nod and never say what I mean. I learned to lie and go to bed with a man I hated, who cared less about my pleasure than the appearance of it. Faking how I felt in and out of bed became second nature to me. So yes, I can do politics with the best of them. I just don't care to do so, if I can help it. I am no longer held hostage by a man more powerful than myself and I have a new goal in mind: find someone to warm my bed who is my choice.

Not just anyone. There are plenty of men who fit Yorian's unimpressive mold. No, I want someone that will keep me satiated with pleasure, while staying interesting enough that I don't want to kick them out of bed immediately after they have done their duty.

No, I want an orc. One of our new overlords, for all that the nobles in this room are still pretending they are the ones in power. They only operate at the discretion of the kingdom of Orik and the treaty that was forged by the marriage of our queen to the orc king.

The same treaty that has me in place as the human Regent of Adrik, acting in proxy for Queen Adalind. But there is also an orc regent, to act in proxy of the orc king Rognar. The king that has my friend Queen Adalind well-pleased in bed and gave me the idea of an orc lover in the first place.

As if my thoughts summoned him, the orc, Regent Verrick, enters the room, the doors booming open with his entrance, and my breath catches slightly.

He's just *so* male. Tall and strong, with rippling green-gray muscles. He is not what would be called handsome, true, with tusks jutting from his lip and tattoos on his forehead and body with obsidian eyes. It does not matter to me. Even his harsh face attracts me. There's something about the constant frown that he sports that calls to me. I want to make him smile or even laugh. Even though both things I cannot quite picture.

The rest of the room goes silent, and studiously ignores him, as if they can make him disappear by not acknowledging his presence. .

Unfortunately for all present, I have no desire for Verrick to leave.

"Warchief Verrick!" I greet him, smiling in welcome, making him frown deeper. Hmm, this amuses me, so I smile even wider, perhaps even a little flirtatiously.

"So good of you to arrive. Is all well with the orcs?"

He nods, his expression staying exactly as unwelcoming as before, and glowers around the room. "The orcs are doing well. Two matings have just occurred at the Garden Manor, one of which is from my clan."

Garden Manor, where willing women can go to meet and match with orcs to mate. The women that go there have lately acquired the nickname among the masses of the War Brides since their willingness to bind themselves to orcs is what stopped the war between Adrik and Orik. I was the coordinator at Garden Manor before I became regent. A murmur runs through the court like lightning. Most of the humans don't like to think of those that are choosing to mate with the orcs. They see it as demeaning. *Fools.*

I clap my hands and say, "How delightful! I'm sure the king and queen will be happy to hear their treaty is already a success."

This silences the murmurs like I knew it would. No one wants to get on the bad side of the queen who saved us all and the king who is very willing to kill anyone who threatens his bride. The House Grimble has already fallen into ruin from trying to go against our rulers. Their lands are currently in holding, waiting to be bestowed upon a deserving noble, which is something else the gossips have been speaking of.

Verrick comes to sit next to me and I give him a little wink as he sits down. This causes him to stumble slightly. The action is so subtle that someone would have to be looking very closely to see his reaction. Which I am. *Adorable.* He is not as immune to me as he pretends.

I continue, "Now that Warchief Verrick is present, let us continue with the matters at hand. The remaining amount of the tribute, where will it come from again?"

The argument erupts once more, the debate raging on. I settle back in my seat, no longer bored now that the object of my interest is next to me. The same could not be said for Verrick, however. He grows more and more tense the more the talking rages on. Under his breath I hear him mutter, "They should just draw swords and be done with it."

"A singular notion," I whisper back, even though he was not speaking to me. "Shall we place bets on who would win? Count Zaimar is quite deft with a blade, but Duchess Kimber can match him easily with rage."

The orc looks at me as if I am a strange thing, a puzzle he cannot solve. I suppose a human has never flirted with him before, but he'll just have to get used to it.

He opens his mouth as if to answer, his pointed ears growing a bit darker, then closes his mouth, stands up as if he did not just sit down, and announces to the room, "I will support whatever Regent Santir decides. Excuse me."

With that, he leaves the room as quickly as he entered, the room staring at me. But I am not thinking of them as I stare at the broad, well-built back exiting the room.

It's already decided. I wanted a lover of my choice and I've found one.

Him.

CHAPTER 2

Verrick

*L*iving among humans will drive me mad. I walk out of the Council Chamber and veer sharply to the left, headed down to the courtyard. I need to train, to drive out my lingering fears and frustrations.

Being in Adrik reminds me of *her*. Lucy. For years I have banished my treacherous former mate from my thoughts, but now that I see her people everywhere, I am plagued by thoughts of her.

Is she somewhere in this godsforsaken kingdom? Was she killed during the war? Or, when she ran off with my family's treasures, did she go somewhere far away where I could never find her? It is likely I'll never know because I will not look for her. She is dead to me.

I enter the courtyard and catch the eye of my second-in-command, Friza. She sees the dark cloud storming above my head and nods, pulling out her ax.

"Need the thoughts knocked out of your head?" she asks, smiling and brandishing her blade. "I can do that for you."

"Your arrogance will get your blood spilled on the sand," I return, glad to think of the upcoming fight and not my troubles.

For there are many. Not just Lucy and the memories I try to keep at bay, but the horrible Council, with all their nattering and whining, and . . . Pellia.

Leave it to a human woman to plague me again. Ever since we first met, she has made her interest clear. I am no fool. I can see her flirting with me. But I swore, *I swore*, never to take another mate. No good can come from it, especially not another human. Even one that is warm and welcoming and . . .

Friza's blade slices through the air and I barely dodge. Right. Naught else exists, but the task at hand.

We spar for a while, neither giving much ground. Orcs are competitive, after all. I am just about to land a glancing blow when a cry interrupts our bout, stilling both our blades.

"Warchief Verrick!"

I turn to see one of my orcs that had been on guard duty. "What is it, Ukiv?"

"There is a mob of refugees from the south at the gates! They are demanding to speak to the regent."

I pause for a moment. This seems like more human problems and I am tempted to send for Regent Santir to deal with it. But mobs can be dangerous. I suddenly imagine Pellia being pulled under a throng of bodies and trampled. She is a small, curvy human, with no muscles to speak of. She would be lost in a trice.

Heavily, I sigh. I suppose it will be up to me, then.

"Friza, Sawak, Ukiv, you're with me. Be ready for trouble if this gets out of hand. I will speak to them."

The warriors I indicated flank my sides, weapons at the ready. If the mob wants trouble, we will give it to them.

As we near the gate, I hear the refugees shouting, "Bring us the regent! They will hear our voices! Bring us the regent!"

I step to the gate and see human soldiers standing at the ready.

One greets me as I approach. "Regent Verrick, I am Cole, captain of the guards. It's looking ugly out there. I can't say that I recommend going out there to speak with them."

I stare stoically at the human captain. "I'll be fine, Captain. Open the gates so that I may speak to them."

He shakes his head. "That is not wise. They could try to

storm the castle."

I open my mouth to order him to obey me when a warm voice interrupts from behind me.

"What is going on?"

Pellia. I thought she would still be in council, but it must have finished. She is exactly who I did not want here.

Captain Cole doesn't seem to have my reservations, however. "Regent Santir, thank the gods you are here. Can you tell Regent Verrick that opening the gates to this mob is not the right thing to do? There are too many people. They could break away, push into the castle; they seem angry enough to do it."

"They would never get past my orcs," I growl, annoyed at being second-guessed.

Pellia looks considering, then smiles, "I'm sure that Warchief Verrick would have everything under control, but have we tried speaking to them through the gate? Asking to speak to their leader about why they are here? I think that would be best rather than having them rush the castle and being slaughtered. Warchief Verrick is right that they would be no match for trained orcs."

Her words are flattering and placating at the same time. It makes me doubt them. Humans often use manipulation to get what they want and Pellia seems better with words than most.

Still, it would not hurt to try her plan. I stride forward to the gate and bark, "Who is your leader? Send them forward now, so that we may speak."

The crowd quiets their yelling, and a murmur runs through them as if trying to decide who to send. Finally, a woman's voice calls, "Are you the regent?"

"I am," I confirm.

"As am I," comes a voice at my side. I look down and see Pellia standing right next to me, looking serene.

The crowd parts and a woman pushes through. She is tall and overly thin, as if she hasn't had a good meal in a while. Her hair is a tangled riot of red and she stands with the bearing of a general.

"We need to speak to you immediately. Open the gates."

"You do not seem peaceful," Pellia counters, "Why would we let you in?"

"Because if you do not, then we will riot in the streets until you do. This is no small matter we come to you with," sneers the woman, clearly unimpressed with both Pellia and me, even with the soldiers at our backing. She is either brave or very stupid. Perhaps just desperate.

"The south is burning," the redhead continues, "and if we do not save it, we are all doomed."

CHAPTER 3

Pellia

T he peasant woman's words are shocking. I need more
information.

"What do you mean, the south is burning?"

"No," replies the woman. "I won't say another word until
you let us in and hear us out. I'm done talking with a gate in my
face."

Her audacity of speaking to nobility like this is almost
impressive. Perhaps a touch foolish, though. She is lucky that I
have such thick skin, and she is not speaking to one like Stella
Kimber. Instead, I say, "I will not let all of you in. You may come,
along with two more representatives, to state your case."

She snorts, "You must think me daft to go in there
with only two people to back me. I'm liable to enter and be
immediately thrown into the dungeons for daring to speak
above my station."

So she knows that her attitude is not wise. Though she is
correct that some might treat her that way, I am annoyed that
she is so suspicious. If I really wanted to hurt her and the mob
that she came with, I would have thrown Verrick and his orcs at
them and I'm sure they could quell the crowd in moments. But
then there would be a lot of dead people on my doorstep and no
solutions.

Wracking my brain, I finally say, "I swear, before Theesia,

Mother Goddess, Patron of Hospitality, that you will be my guests and that no harm will come to you as long as you mean no harm to me and mine. Alright?"

The crowd murmurs. No one invokes Theesia lightly. She is petty about her punishments and brutal in her justice.

Finally, the mob's leader nods. "Alright, I accept in Theesia's name. May she strike you with blight if you are lying."

Verrick stiffens next to me as if insulted on my behalf, but I merely smile at her impudence. "Very well. Captain, let . . ." I pause for her name.

"Bronwyn. Bronwyn Cooper," the woman says.

"Let Bronwyn Cooper and her two associates in. We will meet in the Council Chamber to speak."

With that, I turn and take Verrick's arm in mine, pulling him along. He hesitates for a moment, then follows obediently. *Ah, I do so like that in a male*, I think, and secretly smile at my jest.

We enter the Council Chamber, and Verrick relaxes when he sees it is empty. Poor orc, he truly hates meeting with the Council. I definitely dislike it, but at least I am used to it.

As he escorts me to my seat, he says, "Are you sure you need me?"

Oh yes. I need him for things he cannot even fathom yet. But instead of the innuendo, I say, "They demanded to speak to the regent and you are the regent."

"So are you," he returns. "This seems like a human problem."

That irks me. "If the south is indeed burning, whatever that means, then there is a good chance that we cannot pay the tithe to Orik without catastrophic death during the winter. That will devastate Queen Adalind and if she is unhappy . . ."

Verrick grunts, rather than finishing my thought. He knows what I mean. If my dear friend Adalind is upset, her protective mate, King Rognar, will be angry. That anger cannot bode well for the one he left in charge.

Continuing, I say, "You need to stop thinking of things as 'human problems' or 'orc problems.' They are one and the same now. Our kingdoms are united through ink and blood. What affects one people will now invariably affect the other. I know they left you here mainly to protect the kingdom with your forces, and you are doing the job well, but it is not fair that you keep just leaving everything to me, without so much as giving your input."

He grunts again and I think that is all the response I am going to get when he surprises me by saying, "I thought you would be more comfortable if I kept my distance. I know humans dislike orcs, as a rule."

Well, that *will not do.* I open my mouth to tell him I do not want him to keep his distance at all when the Council Chamber doors open. Captain Cole is escorting Bronwyn Cooper, who is flanked by two men in rough-spun clothing. The other delegates, I assume.

"Bronwyn, welcome," I say, trying to be pleasant, even as the woman stares at me with a frown. "Who are your comrades?"

"This is Quill," she says, gesturing to the first man. "This is Owen." She gestures to the second.

"Well, welcome to the both of you as well. Shall we get started?"

Bronwyn's eyes flick over to Verrick and says, "Does he need to be here? I would prefer we speak alone."

Ah, to the Nether with it. I just told Verrick our kingdoms need to be united and now this disrespect, weakening my position already.

I say, diplomatically, but perhaps a touch peevishly, "Warchief Verrick is the Orikesh Regent. He needs to be present for whatever you want to tell us."

"Fine," she replies mulishly. "But don't blame me when things get ugly."

"Whatever can you mean?"

"Someone is burning the towns and fields in the Southlands and we believe it to be the orcs."

"What?" I am shocked. My eyes flick over to Verrick, who

stands stone-faced, with no reaction in any of his body language. "Do you have proof that orcs are setting these fires?"

"Who else would do it?" counters Bronwyn. "But, yes, we have proof."

One of the men, Owen, pipes up. "We found a piece of an orc warkilt on the ground near one fire and an orc-make knife at another. As far as we can tell, they don't think Adrik suffered enough in the war and want to finish the job they started."

"That makes no sense," I counter. "Orcs are warlike but honorable. They would never slowly starve an enemy that they could face in battle. Is that not so, Warchief Verrick?"

"Orcs do not burn food stores or fields," confirms Verrick. "We take them or cut off delivery routes so the enemy cannot get to them. Food is precious. Why would we destroy it when we can use it?"

"Of course, you would say that now, while you are being confronted," scoffs the man called Quill.

"You forget to whom you speak," I say harshly. Diplomacy be damned. "Warchief Verrick is one of the greatest warriors in Orik, which means he is one of the greatest on the entire continent of Teurilia. Even your whole mob poses no threat to him. If he wanted to kill you for your insolence, he could and there is nothing you nor I could do about it. If his orcs were burning your homes, he would just say so, and what would you do? How could you stop him? He has no reason to lie."

Silence greets my tirade and I can see the peasants are looking hesitant.

I continue, "With merely a thousand orcs, a tiny fraction of their Horde, they decimated our armies, and destroyed a superior force. Each orc is worth a hundred of our soldiers. With their natural strength and stamina, tough hides, and training, they are a force to be reckoned with. If they wanted to destroy us, they could. But they do not, because of the treaty struck between Queen Adalind and King Rognar. They are obedient to their king. So, no, I do not believe that any orcs are the culprits that are setting fires in the south."

Finally, the peasant woman speaks again. "But if orcs are not destroying our food and homes, who is?" Bronwyn demands, "What about the orc artifacts we found?"

"That is the question," I say. "But if it were orcs on a covert mission, they would not be careless enough to leave behind evidence. I would wager that it is someone that wants to sow discord between humans and orcs, and they are succeeding."

"Whatever reason they are doing it doesn't matter," declares Bronwyn. "Winter is a scant three months away, and our stores and crops are being destroyed. If they aren't stopped, we will all starve."

"Then we will stop them," I say evenly.

"How?" scoffs the peasant woman. "By waving your hands and wishing it so? Nobles are as useless as a bucket with a hole when common folk die."

Verrick steps forward, suddenly looming over the redhead. He looks dangerous and stern. "You go too far, human. Regent Santir has been nothing but cordial and understanding to you and yet you take every opportunity to spit it back in her face. Do you want her help or do you want to be thrown out of the castle with an armed escort so that you cannot cause more trouble?"

Bronwyn steps forward, but the hulking figure that is Verrick dwarfs her. They stare each other down for a moment, then the woman seems to deflate. At least it shows she has some sense to not try to fight an orc.

She says tensely, "I'm sorry, Regent. My anger gets the best of me."

The diplomat in me wants to soothe ruffled feelings, but as regent, I cannot do that. When Bronwyn disrespects me, she disrespects my position and Queen Adalind, who gave it to me. I tell her, "Tempers run hot when the stakes are so high and so personal. Still, you would do well to work together, rather than against each other. If you want to be enemies, that will not go well for you."

Bronwyn nods, still not looking happy, but at least she appears to be trying to be civil.

Continuing, I say, "We still have a few mages left with Aspects of water or air, which would be useful in putting out fires. We can send them to the southern towns to help in the event of more fires. They will be spread thin, however, and that's only a stop-gap measure besides. What we really need is to ascertain where the arsonist, or arsonists, will strike next. We need to intercept them."

One of the men shakes his head. "We tried that. The fires are too random."

"Show me on the map." I gesture to the Council Table, where a map of Adrik is carved into the wood.

Bronwyn steps forward, studying the map and she points. "There. The first fires were in Aquilar, just after refugees started going home. We then had more in Kingsbury and Grimblton, right when people were returning there as well. Then here, here, and here. There doesn't seem to be any pattern."

"Hmm," I say, looking at where she is pointing. "You are right. I don't see a pattern either. Unfortunately, there may have to be more fires before we can find out their purpose."

"Their purpose is to hurt the commonfolk," returns Bronwyn. "We need to stop them before we have hundreds, if not thousands, of starving homeless this winter."

"That will not happen," says Verrick. "I will send word to Orik and they will send the Builders Guild. We can get the villages rebuilt before the first snows."

"Not if they keep burning them down." I point out. "We must find them and put pain to their plot."

"And hang them as a warning to those that would hurt so many," Bronwyn agrees grimly.

"We need to send scouts to every town and village in the south, along with the mages. Trained warriors who can see suspicious signs. The only way to stop them is to find them."

"It will leave the forces at the capital strained, but it can be done," Verrick affirms.

"The people won't like it if you send orcs," says Quill. "Most of them still think it's orcs doing it."

"They will just have to get used to it," I say with a smile. "We are a protectorate of Orik now and the Horde is even taking mates from our own people. Orcs will soon be commonplace."

"But they aren't now," insists Bronwyn. "Everyone knows about the orc artifacts. It will just seem that you are sending more orcs to burn down their homes. I'm not even sure we'll be able to calm the crowd in that case."

"What you say is true," Verrick replies evenly. "But there are hardly any human forces left. Even those who survived the war and were released as prisoners are weakened, many through injury. It would take time that we do not have for them to heal completely and regain their strength. If you want the culprits to be caught soon, you will need those who are strong and fast and that would be orcs."

"Perhaps," I say, "you might tell the people that we showed you evidence the artifacts were fake? Or that if it is orcs, they are not of Warchief Verrick's clan? Convince them we want to help."

"You're asking for a lot," Bronwyn says, sighing, "but at the very least you have convinced me. I'll try to do what you ask."

"That is the only way anything will get done," my lips say with a smile, even as I'm slightly annoyed at the common woman's condescending tone. She is haughty for a commoner. "We can reconvene tomorrow to discuss progress and will get the warriors and mages sent to the south in the morning at the latest."

Standing up straight, I give a nod to the guards that escorted the peasant contingent in. "Escort Mistress Cooper and her associates out of the castle. If there's nothing else, I will excuse myself to my chambers. It has been a long day."

Bronwyn executes a clumsy curtsey. "Thank you, Regent Santir, for listening to us. I'll admit that I doubted you would."

"And I'll admit in the old regime it is likely no one would have," I say kindly. "But it is a new day and that is largely thanks to the orcs. You'd do well to remember that."

With that, I sweep from the room, my skirts rustling against the floor. I check over my shoulder and see that Verrick is watching me leave. *Excellent*. I toss an extra swish into my hips before rounding the corner, out of sight.

Give him something to miss, I muse. I'll have him in bed before the month is out.

I enter my rooms, what was once the queen's chambers, and stop. The door swings shut behind me and I look warily around the room. Nothing is out of place, but something feels wrong. I've been trained since I was a child to sense approaching assassins and that feeling of danger is alerted in me now.

I am about to back out towards the door, my right hand reaching for the hidden blade I always carry, when a voice startles me. "Don't scream."

I whirl around but see no one. Did I imagine it? But no, the voice comes again. "Good. You are as obedient as Yorian said you were."

Yorian? What are they talking about? "Who are you?" I demand. "Where are you?"

"Don't worry about that. We can talk more comfortably from here," the voice says easily. "And I am someone that would like to get revenge on behalf of your dead lover. Isn't that something that you want?"

The Cabal. The group that was formed by Yorian and is still secretly working against Adalind. It must be. After all this time of searching, they have come out of the shadows themselves, just to contact me? And they think I am sympathetic to them? They must believe that I had feelings for Yorian, that our affair was mutual. They are wrong, of course. But I must play this right. Agree, but not seem too eager. Try to ascertain their plan.

"Of course I want revenge," I reply. "Yorian was my world. But that's not possible now."

"It could be," responds the voice, "if you work with us."

"Who are you? How can I know I can trust you? You could be an orc, here to test my loyalty to the new regime. If I agree with you, they could send me to the chopping block tomorrow."

"You'll just have to ask yourself what you want most, to be safe and serve the people that killed the love of your life or to get vengeance and free Adrik from their rule."

Whoever the owner of the voice is, they are delusional. Yorian was *not* the love of my life. I hated him with everything I am. But it's useful that they think I would be on their side.

Still, I say, "Give me something, a sign that I can trust you, and I will do whatever you want. If it means that I can help Yorian rest in peace, I would walk to the Nether for you, but I need to know who I am working with."

"We do not use names," says the voice. "I am called Sting and I am but a messenger. I come from the one that has inherited Yorian's will. He has a message to you, from Yorian."

That leaves my blood cold. Yorian left me a message in the event of his death? That should not surprise me. He seeks to control me, even now that he is dead and gone. I keep a neutral expression on my face, but it is difficult to hide how those words make my skin crawl.

Instead, I try to seem eager. "Yorian sent me a message? What is it?"

"It is 'Blossom, we will be together, even beyond death. Keep your loyalty and I will always be with you.'"

Blossom. That was always what Yorian called me when we were alone. No one knew that. Not even Adalind.

"How did you get such a message? Yorian did not talk to anyone before they killed him."

"There have been contingencies in place for years in the event of assassination. You were always meant to help us if Yorian died. So, Pellia Santir, will you help us?"

I gulp. Becoming a spy against the Cabal is risky. Potentially lethal. They will not hesitate to kill me if they find I am working against them. But this is our only lead. Duchess Grimble, the only member of the Cabal we have captured, is holding up surprisingly well to interrogation and torture. It may be months before she breaks, if ever. In the meantime, the Cabal will have time to rally their supporters and carry out their plans to kill Adalind and Rognar. Not to mention the trouble in the south that, now that I think on it, I am sure is connected to them.

"Alright," I hear myself say. "Tell me your plan."

CHAPTER 4

Pellia

The next morning, I walk up to Verrick on the training grounds and say, "I need to talk to you." Belatedly, I realize we are in front of his orcs and add, "Warchief Verrick," at the end.

He gives me that stare that says he doesn't know what to make of me, then says, "I am in the middle of training. If it is the Council..."

"It is not the Council. But it is important and it cannot wait." I soften my tone and say, "Please. Come with me on my morning ride. We can talk then and you can still get your exercise. It has been a while since you've gone out on your warbeast, has it not?"

His stare does not change, but finally, he nods and says, "Alright. A ride, then."

Good. We need to get out from these prying eyes.

"Excellent," I say. "I'll meet you at the castle gate."

I give him my usual smile and walk away toward the stables.

I love this place. It is warm and light, and yes, smells lightly of horse dung. But I do not care. I have always been safe here, in the stables. Safe from my father's temperamental rages and Yorian's unwelcome favors. Here, the only thing they care about is that you treat your mount right and I do. I go to my old mare,

Zephyr, and pet her white nose.

"Hello, girl," I murmur, my voice sweet, "Did you miss me? Yes? Shall we go for a ride, then?"

Zephyr is already saddled, the stablemaster anticipating my usual ride. Deftly, I swing up, sitting atop my mount like I was born up there. I love being atop my horse. Up here, everything makes sense. The world can fade away, and I can be one with my mount, running with the wind.

I guide Zephyr to the gate and find Verrick already waiting for me. He must have hurried to meet me. Though I know he came merely because of business, I am still warmed by his presence. And such a presence it is, atop his warbeast, looking like something out of an old tale. True, he would have been the villain of an old Adrikian tale, but he would have been one that inspired awe and reverence from the listener. A dangerous threat.

Would that his danger was leashed for me, I think. I saw how the orc king treated my friend Adalind when they were together. A dangerous warrior, a ravening beast, but leashed and tamed for his mistress. I want that for me, at least in a lover. A husband is another matter and not something I want.

"Shall we ride?" I call as I approach.

Verrick merely nods, a grim, brief movement. He is likely confused and maybe even annoyed by my request, but I am unworried by his attitude. He'll understand soon enough.

We move out from the gate, the one that just yesterday was swarmed by the mob. Bronwyn must have kept her promise, because today it is clear. Who is she, this peasant woman that seems to wield such respect and power over her fellow commonfolk? I'll have to write to Adalind and have her spies look into it.

Before long, we are out of the capital, in the fields that surround it, and I give Verrick a cheeky grin, "Shall we race to the edge of the Royal Grove?"

"That would not be wise," he frowns.

I laugh. "That is why it will be fun."

At the close of my words, I nudge Zephyr sharply and she breaks into a gallop.

I feel at peace and free for the first time in ages, racing over the green like this. There is no Council out here, no responsibilities, or plots, or Cabals. Just open air and the wind in my hair.

Behind me, I hear a curse, and then a warbeast is suddenly at my side. I expect him to outpace me quickly. After all, his mount is much bigger and younger than mine. But Verrick stays with me, completely apace. Not a race then, just two riders at high speed.

I flash a smile at him and see him glower in response. I merely laugh, though. How can he be so adorable with his poor attitude? I do not know, but he is to me. It is interesting because Yorian was always smiles and smoothness on the surface, with frightening moodiness below. One would think I would be done with moodiness because of it, but Verrick is different. The opposite of Yorian, I think. I sense a gentleness beneath his frowns. We finally reach the treeline of Royal Grove and we stop. I am breathing hard from my speedy ride, but Verrick looks much the same as before, his face stone.

"You did not race," I laughingly accuse, stretching my back.

"I do not have time for orcling games," he replies simply, "and I am the only one out here with you. I cannot protect you if I leave you behind me."

The statement is arrogant and brusk. Even so, I see that vein of gentleness I suspect in him. He is focused on my protection, not my censure. And though I can tell he does not approve of my childish game, he does not seek to stop or control me, either. More and more I know he is the one I want in my bed.

"Very well," I agree amicably. "No more games then. There is a reason I wanted you out this far."

"And that is?"

"Last night, the Cabal contacted me." I know Rognar briefed him on the Cabal and their sadism, and his entire body tenses at their mention.

"What happened?" he asks sharply. "Were you hurt?"

"I am well," I say, warmed by his concern. "I never actually saw anyone. They spoke to me from a secret chamber that is attached to my room. I searched for the entrance this morning, but could not find it. But there must be a whole labyrinth of secret corridors in the castle that they used to get there. That's why I wanted to have this conversation here, out where we can speak freely without being overheard. The castle is compromised, for now."

"They have a way to get to your room? They could have captured you, or worse. This is no laughing matter, Regent Santir."

"That is not the concern right now, and I am not laughing," I say. "And please call me Pellia when we are alone. It makes me feel like my father is over my shoulder when you use the Santir name."

"How is that not the concern? They could have taken you as a political prisoner or killed you to make a statement. This should be reported to the king and queen immediately."

"Exactly," I retort. "They could have at any time, but they haven't. Because they have gotten it into their heads that I am sympathetic to them."

Verrick stills. "And why would they think that?"

"Because Yorian was delusional. He circulated to everyone that we were childhood sweethearts, destined lovers, all that rot. The actual story is that Yorian could stand no one having something he didn't, and he wanted me because he had a rival who wanted me as well. Also, because my mother was from Sheaotha across the sea, I was an exotic, rare thing he desired for his collection. I won't pretend that he didn't treat me much better than everyone else in his circle and that he even believed his own story, but I never loved him. I was with him because my father feared what would happen to House Santir if we had said no. He was always more concerned with our family's power than my well-being."

The speech pours out of me like festering pus from an

infected wound. I do not speak of that time with Yorian if I can help it. It was hard, going to bed with a man I did not love and pretending to care for him under fear for my life. Over ten years of putting on a mask so that I could live, all while hating him every second. But it doesn't do to dwell on it. I only want to move on.

"But the Cabal believes the story that you were in a love match with the king?" Verrick asks carefully, breaking my reverie.

"Yes," I reply. "They think I mourn him and that they can use me to carry out their newest plan."

"What is the plan?"

"They plan to lay a trap for you in the south. It is *them* setting the fires. They mean to lure you to a lair they have in Grimblton. Their agent told me they have a plan that will expel the orcs from Adrik, and that taking you captive is the key to it working."

"Why do they need me? If they think of making me a hostage, it would never work. If they try to use me to threaten Orik, my king would merely send more of the Horde and start killing all the nobles until he found the right ones."

"That may be their plan. They did not say. If it is, then at the very least it could reignite the war, an outcome they already tried for when they tried to kill the queen and king during their Bride Chase last month. Several of the nobles are rich enough to hire private armies, maybe even ogre mercenaries from across the Abyssal Ocean. There would be blood and slaughter and innocent lives would be lost. But, like I said, they didn't tell me any specifics. Just that they need you to be lured to the south."

"How does burning the towns in the south accomplish that? It is a problem, to be sure, but not one that I would attend to myself. I have already sent the orc scouts to investigate and find the perpetrators. I was never planning on going with them."

"I know. That is why they contacted me. I am supposed to pull you in and get you directly involved. We need to have it appear as if I am doing that very thing. If they think we are following their plan, then what we really can do is set our own trap for them. When you are in the south and reach the township of Grimblton, they plan for me to drug you so that they can take you. But what if we only pretended to do so? Then when the Cabal comes to take you as their hostage, we could capture them instead. We could get them all in one fell swoop. At the very least we would get some of their highest lieutenants."

Verrick nods. "A sound strategy, but should we not contact Urim, the King's Shield, and your Dame Zera? The king left them in charge of the investigation into the Cabal."

"But we have no time," I argue. "And they obviously have spies in the palace. They could get to me in my own chamber, for all the gods' sakes."

"A detail I have not forgotten and do not like," my companion growls.

"Precisely. Finding out that we have sent for help would be child's play to them. They knew details about our schedules and Council meetings that they should not. We have no way of knowing how far their information network extends. If we were to send a falcon with a message now, there is a high probability they would discover it and its contents. Then they would know that I am not actually on their side. As of now, they consider me an easily used pawn in their schemes, Yorian's grief-stricken mistress. I have to appear to be following their plan exactly for us to be able to lay a trap."

"But you are not grief-stricken?"

I scoff. "Gods, no. Like I said, I wished for Yorian to die longer than anyone. Destroying his Cabal will be my ultimate revenge against him. To erase him and his influence completely from Adrik."

"Then, I suppose, for now, we can follow your plan. The more associates of the Cabal we capture, the easier it will be to dismantle them."

"Exactly. There is one other thing, though," I venture, feeling both excited and nervous at the thought of telling him.

"What is it?" he asks.

"The part of the plan they want me for . . . specifically what they've ordered me to do in order to lure you south. They want me to seduce you so that your guard will be down when I give you the drug in Grimblton."

"What?" he says, looking for all the world like a startled deer.

"Yes, in order for the plan to work, we are going to have to pretend to be lovers."

CHAPTER 5

Agony

C heerful sunlight pours into the ritual chamber of the tower, at odds with the dark scene in front of me, when the messenger falcon arrives, a missive from Sting attached to its talons. It is done. We have pulled Pellia into the plot. Sting reports she seemed eager. She wants revenge against the orcs as much as we do, though for different reasons. She will be easily controlled, a useful tool in our plan.

I didn't want to bring her into our scheme, but we have no other way of luring the orc regent to the south without her words in his ear. Her body in his bed, addling his thoughts until it is too late. I wince at that thought, Pellia in bed with an orc. I hate that part of the plan, but Sting is right. We are at war and sacrifices need to be made in order to ensure our victory. For though the ritual we plan can be done with any orc, I believe the more powerful the sacrifice we prepare, the more power we will receive. So the orc regent is key and Pellia is imperative to capturing him. Luckily, the lady didn't ask too many questions, being as willing to please as Yorian always bragged she was.

My hands curl into the armrest of my chair, crushing the missive as I do so. Anger curls in my belly. She should have been mine! Pellia was always *meant* to be mine. If she had been then maybe I wouldn't have developed the . . . appetites that I have. The depravities. I know the things I need to feel whole are not . . . savory. No matter. She'll be made to understand, as I was, the necessity of the work done by the Cabal. When she is mine, after this is all over, I'll enjoy educating her and purifying her body of the stench of the orc before I take her.

A muted scream echoes through the ritual chamber, interrupting my thoughts. In front of me, the scene pulls me back into the present. Ache and Anguish, my favorite torturers, stand in front of the young man tied to the torture cross. I've already forgotten his name and where he's from. Was he the blacksmith's apprentice or the farmhand? It doesn't really matter. Who or what he was is no longer of consequence, only the attributes that the ritual we've begun has demanded. He's handsome, young, and healthy. Or at least he was before we started in on him. Now he's nothing but the first sacrifice. A model innocent. They've carved him up as the man wails behind his gag, his once-perfect skin in ribbons, blood flowing down to be captured in a basin under his feet, collecting the liquid for the first stage of the ritual we are attempting. This is just the first of the many innocents we will need to torture. The runes they carve into his flesh are an offering to Grazrath, Lord of Pain, dedicating the young man's soul to his service. It is his blessing we are seeking through our work.

With that blessing, we will soon have the strength we need to expel the orcs from Adrik and punish the queen who gave our country to the beasts.

I merely need to bide my time until the orc regent and his ilk are here. Once Pellia brings him to me, then the true fun can begin.

CHAPTER 6

Verrick

"Y ou and I? Lovers?" I ask, both a deep longing and terror rising in me at the thought. Images assail me, unbidden, yet unstoppable. Flawless brown skin under my fingertips, my thrum reverberating in the air. A sigh, or maybe a moan as she takes me, the perfect clasp of her tight heat.

"We do not have to be lovers in truth," she is saying, breaking into my rebellious thoughts as if she had not just lit my world on fire. "But we should pretend that you are falling for my charms. Which, of course, you aren't." That last phrase she softens with a wink, as if she doesn't believe her own words. I am not sure I do either.

She looks beautiful, out here in the sunshine, plotting. The light shines off of her braids and gleams on her smooth, dark skin. Pellia sits astride on her aging mount and looks for all the world like a goddess about to lead her troops into battle. Or tempt an orc to sin.

But she is a goddess I cannot worship. Even as I long to.

Lucy, I remind myself, *think of Lucy.*

She continues, oblivious to my thoughts, "We'll have to tell everyone that I convinced you that we should take a tour of the south, to survey the damage. On the way there, we can make it appear as if we are sharing a tent and you can act as if I am leading you along by the nose. But then when we get to Grimblton and they come to collect your drugged self, we will spring our surprise attack on them."

"Is this farce entirely necessary? We could just pretend that you convinced me to go south with the troops and you could stay in the capital."

"It is extremely necessary," Pellia argues hotly. "Otherwise, who will swap out the drugs they give with a harmless draught? No, we must appear to be following their plan to the letter so that they suspect nothing until it is too late."

"But . . ."

"There can be no arguments," she insists, drawing her mount closer to mine. My warbeast shuffles slightly at the intrusion, but I reach out to place a hand on his neck to keep him calm. Pellia's hand then reaches out, putting her fingers atop mine. My heart kicks in my chest. How can something, *someone*, so small affect me so easily?

"Please, can you not just trust me?" she gazes up at me earnestly, and I have the impulse to wrench her off of her mount and pull her onto mine. *Foolishness.* "You know I am right. This is our chance to pull as many of the Cabal out of the shadows as we can in one fell swoop. Dame Zera is having no luck interrogating Duchess Grimble."

It is true the human knight has not gotten more names of the secretive Cabal from the treacherous Duchess' lips. Apparently, they all wear cloaks and masks when they meet and only address each other in code, so even though the Queen had many run-ins with them during her first marriage she could only suss out the identity of one who is dead now. And though the King was able to capture the Duchess, the Cabal's agent, before she killed the Queen, she has been like a monk with a vow of silence. No matter what they do to her, she will not talk. The King's spymaster, Urim, has been there with Dame Zera working on the prisoner as well and, though I know he has no scruples, even he has failed.

Pellia is right. This is a chance that has fallen in our laps.

Her plan is sound. When the agents come to kidnap me, they will find themselves taken and imprisoned instead. Still, it goes against my very nature to trust a human woman, even one as open as Pellia. *But my king trusts her*, I remind myself for the umpteenth time. That needs to be good enough for me.

Finally, I sigh, "When will we leave?"

The human smiles at me, radiantly. It makes her appealing nature blinding. But I will remain hardened against it. *I hope.*

"I see no reason to wait. Grimblton is far in the south, several day's journey even if we ride hard, and we will have to stop along the way to make appearances at many of the other affected towns to keep up our story. We can also pass out relief supplies and tally losses—which will be useful anyway for planning for winter."

I am amused by Pellia's mind which flits from topic to topic. "Always a plan within a plan for you, is it not?"

She merely grins, before running her fingers through her braids and then dropping her fingers to the laces of her dress.

Alarmed, I rear back. "What are you doing?"

My brusk question does not offend Pellia, and she merely responds, "I am rumpling myself. I was meant to be seducing you on this ride, the beginning of me having my wicked way with you, so when we get back to the castle, I must look the part. If I look too put-together the Cabal's agent that visited me last night will be suspicious that I am not following their plan. We should rumple you too."

As she talks, the human woman slightly loosens her laces, pulls the shoulder of her gown askew, and wrinkles the bottom of her gown with her fists. When she is done, Pellia looks like she was hastily put together after a quick tryst. *She is good at these games of subterfuge*, I realize.

I ask, "Have you been a spy before?"

She shakes her head, still smiling, "I merely have experience in showing the world what they expect to see. It kept me alive longer. Now, rumple yourself. Or would you like my help?"

She says these last words playfully, her smile growing flirtatious. She is not shy about what she wants, this human. It is just a pity that she seems to want the one orc that *cannot* give her what she so obviously desires.

"I can do it myself," I say back sternly, trying to dissuade her advances. But she merely shrugs and waits, no inkling that she might be put off by my rejection. With deliberation, I copy her movements from before, running my finger through my hair, skewing the straps of my weapons slightly and undoing my belt partially.

I feel a little hot at the thought of Pellia watching me do these actions, as I watched her, but when I look up she is looking away respectfully and I find I am . . . disappointed. How odd. *How maddening.* This is why beautiful human women are so dangerous. They turn my head until I know not what is up or down, left or right. None of my reactions are what they should be.

When I finish, I clear my throat. Pellia looks back at me, her smile growing.

"You look perfect," she says, practically purring. "Everyone will talk once we get back. And when we announce we are going on a tour of the south and then share a tent together, it will set even more tongues wagging."

I merely nod at her words, still a little thrown by my inner turmoil.

Then I ask, "Who should be told about this plot?"

She cocks her head to one side. "Must we tell anyone else? The more people who know, the more likely we are to be found out. Who else did you want to tell?"

"My second-in-command Friza should know. She is sharper than most and would probably see through our ruse. She isn't one to watch her words very closely and might expose our playacting if we do not bring her into our circle. A few of my most trusted orcs, the ones that would be most suspicious of me taking a human lover. Especially since you will not smell like you have had sex with an orc."

Pellia frowns. "Smells? Will that be a problem? We cannot tell *all* of your orcs that are coming with us. No offense intended, but I cannot imagine that all of them have the acting skills necessary to keep up the facade we need."

I grimace. "My clan is not one that delves deeply into subterfuge, it's true. We are as we appear. I suppose there are ways to mimic the smells, to make it appear that I am at least pleasuring you, even if we are not fully committing the act . . . but you would have to arouse the right scents . . . by touching yourself."

She shrugs, looking not at all surprised or scandalized by my suggestion. "That is done easily enough. Though it is almost sounding like it would be easier if we just had sex."

Flustered, I say severely, "That cannot happen."

Pellia responds to my harshness with a mischievous grin. "I know, I know. I am merely joking, Verrick. We will do nothing that will make you uncomfortable. Trust me."

As if I will not be uncomfortable being in the same tent as a beautiful woman touching herself, becoming fragrant in her arousal. Not just any beautiful woman, but the flirtatious Pellia. I am becoming half-hard just thinking about it, to my ever-lasting chagrin.

Not noticing my dangerous thoughts, Pellia claps her hands together. "Alright, so that is what we'll do. You'll tell a small, *very small*, group about our plan, but the rest of everyone else we'll fool as best we can. We have no way of knowing how many spies the Cabal has in the castle and secret listening spots. Or how many people they will plant in our touring party. We should tread carefully and you should tell those that you are informing in Orikesh. I doubt any in the Cabal have bothered to learn your tongue."

"They could have a language stone," I point out.

Pellia frowns, a strange expression to see on her normally sunny face. "That is true. Do you have a silence totem?"

The question opens old wounds, as I think of the reason my clan lost their silence totem. *Lucy, thrice-damn you wherever you are.* "No," I say aloud. "My clan doesn't have one."

"Damn," swears Pellia adorably, "I wish we had time to track one down, but time is against us. We'll merely have to be careful and hope that they don't have a language stone."

"I'll be discreet, as will the orcs I tell."

"I'm sure you will be," she assures me. "Well, let us return. If we are to leave by this afternoon, we have much to do."

Pellia smiles again, in that mischievous way. "Race back?"

Before I can groan, she's already taken off, galloping across the open plain. I send my warbeast into a run, once again chasing her so that I might catch up. I am both annoyed by her recklessness and drawn to her free spirit. More inner turmoil.

The chase tries to stir my Mating Instinct, but I hold it tight like a ravening dog on a leash. I will control myself. No matter how tempting the prize.

❋ ❋ ❋

Hours later we are traveling and I am awed by how quickly Pellia pulled together our caravan. Servants rushed to do her bidding, and even a healer and a mage were found to be added to our party. Two rare finds. The healer because only elves and half-elves have healing magic and they don't often leave the confines of the elvish country Arisil. The mage joining was quite the boon since we killed most of the mages during the recent war and the rest were sent south this morning with scouts. It speaks to Pellia's organizational skills that she was able to scrounge up both for our supposed relief mission. We were packed up and ready to go by noon and began our trek south soon after, just like she said. I have known generals who were not as effective at mobilizing people as Pellia is.

She somehow also found Bronwyn and her two lackeys, whose names I do not care to remember, and made them part of the processional. "They're to be advisors," she tells me with a smile, as they are most informed about the situation at hand.

More smoke and mirrors, of course. Everything Pellia is

doing is to appear as if she was following the orders of the Cabal and pulling the wool over my eyes. Hopefully, it works. The life expectancies of spies that play both sides are not long. The idea of the Cabal killing or punishing Pellia in any way sits sourly in my stomach, like rotten meat.

Our travel is uneventful, so in the late evening, we stop in the Umber Wood to camp for the night. My orcs set up my tent and then, brazen as she could be, Pellia orders, "Perfect. Now, Captain Yesri, put my things into Warchief Verrick's tent."

The human captain hesitates, and the bustle of the camp seems to freeze at her words. Pellia has decided against discretion, I see.

Captain Yesri says, "Ma'am? The tent?"

"Is there pixie pollen in your ears, captain? My things need to go into Warchief Verrick's tent. Is that not correct, Warchief Verrick?"

Not trusting myself to speak aloud, I nod, knowing that my expression looks severe and is not helping Pellia's ruse, but unable to do anything about it. I am not comfortable with games of deception.

"You've joined the War Brides, Regent Santir?" questions the human captain, the man obviously confused.

"I never said that," snips Pellia, growing haughty. "What I said was my things need to go into the warchief's tent. Unless that task somehow escapes you?"

"No ma'am. Excuse my impertinence." With that, the captain barks an order and Pellia's substantial trunks are loaded into my tent. It is a good thing I am a Warchief, I muse, or my tent would not be big enough.

Not that it actually matters if her things fit, as this is all for show. Of course.

The camp rises around us, tents going up and campfires being lit. Food is cooked and I stand in line with the rest of my orcs to get it. I try to show at all times that I am a soldier like them, no better or worse.

I expect Pellia to stay in the tent and wait for a servant to bring her repast, but I am surprised as I get to the head of the line that Pellia is laughing while serving food to my orcs. As I stand in front of her, she smiles, her eyes glittering in the setting sun.

"Stew?" she says, offering out the ladle.

I put out my bowl silently, and she fills it with the meat and vegetables from the cauldron over the fire. Pellia winks as she serves me and I feel my ears heat, even as I keep my face impassive. Since we decided to play at being lovers, her flirting has gotten even more bold and I don't know how to react to it.

Friza comes up at my side, eyebrows raised. "Never thought I'd see the day a human highborn lady serves an orc dinner."

The dig makes my hackles rise and I almost growl at Friza when Pellia just laughs again and fills Friza's bowl.

"I was head of Garden Manor for many years and ran that house the whole time. This is not the first time I've served food to make sure that people are fed on time and I dare say it will not be the last."

She smiles prettily at my second-in-command and I have to stop myself from being jealous at the little regent's beauty being directed at someone else. I have no right to jealousy. She is not mine and I am not hers. I merely take my food and sit with my orcs. Friza stays with Pellia, talking to her for a while before coming over with the rest of us. She gives me a curious look and then glances at the human woman, but I don't reply. Friza knows the relationship starting between me and Pellia is fake. I told her and a small group of my most trusted lieutenants what was happening before we left, outside the castle gates, just to be safe. I know she won't say anything, but that doesn't mean she doesn't want to comment. But what happens between the human and me, even if it is all fake, stays between the human and me. I don't need the opinions and playful ribbing of my comrades.

Soon it is dark, dinner is over, and Pellia and I are in the tent, the lumen crystals lit. Pellia sits on a bench, rubbing oils into her deep brown skin, and then begins to carefully massage some cream into her scalp. The scent of the oils and cream lingers heavily in the air, mingling with her own natural scent and the effect is pleasant.

The moment feels intimate. *Too* intimate, as I sit on the bed and watch Pellia complete her bedtime routine. *Domestic* is the word. I cannot risk being domestic with the beautiful human. It feels too much like a relationship. One that will open me to betrayal again.

Instead, I stand, pulling the largest blanket off of my pile of furs, beginning to affix it to the tent poles, bisecting the space.

"What are you doing?" she asks, behind me.

I turn to her and see that she has tied her braids up on her head and wrapped them with a scarf of silk.

"I'm giving us privacy," I say severely, turning on her my most fearsome frown. It does not seem to have any effect, though, as she cocks her head to the side with curiosity.

"Whatever for? We are lovers after all," Pellia gives me a winsome smile. Always keeping up with the ruse. I suppose someone could be listening to us, even now. But I know I need to keep my distance from her, even if that distance is as thin as a blanket.

"I require solitude for my evening meditations," I bluff, knowing the words sound silly coming from my mouth. Yet, Pellia nods.

"Alright, if you insist. But do not take too long. I have appetites that need sating. As do you." Her voice becomes a seductive purr at the end. Then she looks at me and mouths some words. It takes me a moment to discern their meaning.

Play along.

I sigh, but summon a growl to my voice. "You will not wait long."

She smiles at me, that same sunny expression that she gives so freely, then sidles up along my front, trailing her fingers over my chest before disappearing behind the blanket.

My skin is on fire where she touched me, burning with painful desire. I do not think I have ever wanted a female as badly as I do the maddening coquette with whom I am currently sharing a tent. Hurriedly I douse the lumen crystals, leaving us in darkness. There is no way that I can share a bed with Pellia. Especially if she is going to touch herself this night. Her scent will be too close, her body temptingly near, her willing spirit calling to mine with open abandon.

I will sleep on the ground. It will not be the first time. When I was an orcling, I often slept out under the stars on the rocky dirt as part of my training. I can do so now without complaint. I go to lie down when I hear a moan from behind the makeshift curtain.

"Oh . . . Verrick."

Oh no. She is going to be . . . vocal with her . . . endeavors. It comes again, this time accompanied by the sounds of movement in the furs.

"Yes, Verrick! There, oh, there!"

I am frozen on the ground, listening to Pellia's moans and sighs. Her scent blooms in the close space, and I know she is touching herself. To thoughts of me? Or is it still a part of our charade?

"Verrick, oh, Verrick! So good! So, so good! Verrick!"

I begin to harden beneath my warkilt. I cannot help it. I can see her, in my mind's eye, touching herself to add to the ruse that we are together. She is bare in my vision, her braids fighting to escape from the silk wrap she put them in, her legs splayed open, one hand between her thighs and the other on a dusky nipple. I can see her smiling at me in invitation, her legs falling further apart.

She whines, a needy sound, weaving in time to the vision in my mind, and I cannot help it. My fist finds my cock, squeezing with a brutal grip, seeking for some relief. Unintelligible sounds come from Pellia's mouth, going higher and higher as she seeks her peak. I give my cock a harsh pump, a cheap imitation of what it really wants.

Breathy whimpers intermingle with shouts and moans and on a high-pitched shriek of my name, Pellia comes, the scent of her lust exploding in the air around us. I do as well, barely making it into the chamber pot before my seed can splash all over the ground. The scent of our arousal mixes in that air and it smells good. Like sweet, willing woman, and raw fucking.

So wrapped up am I in the last vestiges of daydream that it takes me a moment to realize that everything has gone silent. and a light snore comes from the other side of the blanket. I realize in horror that Pellia means to finish here.

Stalking past the curtain to the furs, I lean over her sleeping form. She lays still; her wrap perfectly tied, her nightdress slightly askew on her shoulder. How can anyone fall asleep so quickly? Especially after such a release?

"What are you doing?" I hiss.

She jerks awake, startled, and I press my hand over her mouth so that she does not make a sound of shock. When she remains silent, big, dark eyes blinking at me over my large hand, I slowly remove it.

"Verrick?" she whispers, questioning. "What are you doing here?"

"You can't stop there," I whisper back.

"What do you mean?"

"Orcs have . . . high stamina. You cannot stop here without making me look like a laughingstock."

"High stamina? For sex?"

"For fucking," I confirm, still whispering. "If you want to make it look like we had sex tonight, fine. But you will have to go on longer."

She narrows her eyes, suspicious. "How much longer?"

I shrug. "Until at least dawn."

"Dawn?" She almost says the word aloud in her incredulity, before correcting to a whisper. "You cannot tell me that orcs fuck their partners for that long. It beggars belief!"

"Most would for longer. Once an orc starts fucking, the Mating Instinct would almost invariably take hold. It pushes us to breed. We go until every drop of our seed is gone."

Now it is Pellia's turn to sigh. "Well, I don't suppose you could help me, if I am to stay up that long after riding all day?"

"I cannot," I say solemnly.

She sighs again. "No, I suppose you *will* not. But what else did I expect? Alright. Well, I hope you can sleep through noise, because I am noisy and you are going to be hearing your name. A lot."

I nod, not sure if she is being sarcastic or not, but I answer just in case. "I will do my best. Thank you, Regent Santir."

"Pellia," she grouses back. "Pellia, damn you, if I am to get no sleep tonight."

"Pellia," I agree. "Thank you."

Then I beat a hasty retreat to the other side of the barrier, just in time to hear her begin again, with a sweet whimper and moan.

It's going to be the longest, most torturous night of my life.

Yet somehow, there's no place else I'd rather be.

CHAPTER 7

Pellia

My eyes burn with the sandy feeling of not enough sleep as they open to the pale light of early morning. I kept my promise and pleasured myself until dawn, shouting my lungs out. My last few orgasms were hard won, tired as I was, but I wrung them out somehow. I very much doubt the rest of the camp thinks well of me. But I saved Verrick's pride and established us as lovers.

The moment the sky began to lighten, however, I let myself fall asleep. The hubbub of the camp breaking their fast and breaking camp has awoken me scant hours later. Riding the rest of the day will be a challenge. Perhaps I can talk Verrick into letting me ride with him so that I can doze. It will further cement our ruse and let me get closer to him, all at the same time.

Perhaps I should be more self-conscious that I touched myself and made myself come while Verrick listened, but I'm not. I'm a practical sort and it needed to be done. There is perhaps a small part of me that is disappointed that Verrick didn't join me. A small part that hoped that he would be tempted. But he remained stoic as ever, even as he told me that orcs fuck their partners all night. *That* is interesting knowledge to have, to be sure.

The thought is immediately followed by discomfort in my bladder, and I rise to relieve it. I peek around the hanging blanket and see that Verrick is already gone, no trace that he ever slept on the ground. As long as the blanket isn't still hanging. I tug it down and toss it carelessly on the furs. There. Anyone who looked in the tent would assume that we spent a very loud night together. But he could be back any second and I very much do not wish to be caught on the chamber pot when he does. That will not help in my quest to actually seduce the surly Warchief.

Putting on a dressing gown and slipping on slippers, I exit the tent. No one is looking my way as I emerge, and I can slip into the woods without being spotted. Good. I stop behind a tree, but the idea of someone catching me in my vulnerable state stops me. Further, then. Where no one will accidentally find me.

I move through the trees until I hear the babbling of a brook and stop behind a large rock. I go to relieve myself and am just finishing when I hear a light splash.

I freeze.

What was that? I hastily finish fixing my clothes before I peek around the boulder.

What I see makes my mouth go dry. The brook burbles into a pond and the pond has a very naked orc in it; Verrick. He is washing himself, his back to me, but the water only goes up far enough to cover his thighs. Taut buttocks are clearly visible, leading to a muscular back, each rippling bulge moving in a sinuous rhythm as he washes himself. From my vantage point, I see his hands moving, and they seem to move down his front toward his cock.

I duck down into the bushes, not watching the intimate moment any longer. It would be wrong to watch him in his state of undress without his consent. Still, unbidden, my breathing speeds up and I gasp a little at the memory of all of his delicious naked skin and muscles.

The little sound is a mistake.

"Who goes there?" demands Verrick's silky voice, an edge to his tone.

Curses, I forgot about orc hearing. I consider trying to crawl away, but he would probably give chase, thinking me an enemy. I could speak as bashfully as I am feeling, but that is not really my style.

Instead, I put on a cheerful voice and call, "Not to worry, 'Tis I, Pellia."

"Pellia?" he chokes incredulously. "What are you doing out here?"

I am not going to tell him I was relieving myself after sleeping. So a half-truth it is. "I heard a sound and came to investigate it. I didn't mean to find you . . .like this."

"You heard a sound and went to investigate by *yourself*?" His tone is incredulous again and slightly disapproving, neither of which I appreciate.

So I say, "It was only a small sound, and I was very quiet. You wouldn't have caught me if you were not an orc."

"So you would have been fine with finding another orc?"

Only if they were as attractive as you, I flirt inwardly. But I know he wouldn't appreciate such an answer. Alternatively, I state, "Well, I wasn't to know it was an orc, was I? Or a person of any kind. You could have been a creature, like a deer." *Or a bear*, I finish inside lamely. My half-truth is making me sound foolish. Going after a sound by myself really is not the safest of ideas.

Verrick seems to agree with my unspoken thoughts. He says, from a much closer distance, "You should not go off by yourself, Regent Satir. You are an important figure and should be protected at all times."

He's right, of course, annoyed as I am with his formality. I turn to tell him so and find that he is standing right beside me. His kilt is back on, dagger strapped to chest, ax on his back. But his skin is still wet, and he looks *lickable*.

I smile at the thought, enjoying the casual sensuality of my thoughts. I have never really experienced true desire and I find I *like* it.

Oblivious, Verrick continues his lecture, "There are many manner of creatures in these woods. What if you had happened on a unicorn and it had carried you off to be its bride?"

That makes me laugh. "Unicorns only carry off maidens. I

am in no danger."

The tall orc looks adorably confused. I explain, "Unicorns like maidens. I have shared a man's bed before, so they would have no interest in me."

"Pah," dismisses Verrick, as if I have said something ridiculous. "A beautiful woman is a beautiful woman."

Warmed at his praise, I preen on the inside. There is no doubt in my mind that he meant it, but also no doubt that he did not mean to say it. So I don't call focus to his slip, only storing it for later and say, "Well, in that case, I would scream and you would extricate me from my trouble, I'm sure."

He frowns, looking surly, and replies, "Unicorns are fast. You would be well away before I could arrive."

"You would catch it. I have every faith."

He insists, "No, once a unicorn has its bride, it dances on the wind and is away before anyone can stop it. I would have no chance and you would be taken."

"Then you would hunt it and me down, I am sure, and take me back. All would be well."

He begrudgingly agrees, "I would hunt it, but it would be better if you hadn't been taken in the first place and . . ." He trails off, looking at my smiling face and instantly shutters again, looking irritated. "Are you making jests at my expense?"

I lightly laugh and cautiously reach out a comforting hand to his crossed arms. He does not stop me from touching him, though he focuses down on my hand.

"Ah, Warchief Verrick, I am not making jests. I am teasing, a completely different thing. And you are right, these woods and this journey could be dangerous and I should be more careful. In the future, I promise to go find you or another orc and let them know if I hear anything suspicious without investigating it myself, alright?"

"Finding me should be sufficient," he murmurs, still staring at my hand. His pupils are a little larger than before, threatening to swallow his already dark eyes.

I smile radiantly. He wants me. I know it. I wonder if he

does? No matter, I will show him and we will be lovers soon.

"Alright," I reply, taking my hand back and turning back to the camp. "Just you, then. But, if anything were to happen, remember, I have put my trust in your rescue. You'll have to come after me."

And then I walk back to camp, looking forward to the day of traveling next to my soon-to-be lover.

CHAPTER 8

Verrick

She trusts me. The thought should not be arousing, and yet it is. Pellia rides just behind me, in a protected spot in our riding formation, but though I cannot see her, all my thoughts are of her.

The thought of her being taken by some mysterious party infuriates me. She is right. I would hunt her down and bring her back. But because she is my co-regent and a friend to my queen or something else? I cannot say for certain.

Deep within me I can feel the Mating Instinct stir and I bid it back to sleep through my will alone. Pellia is not for me. She can't be. I swore an oath never to be taken in by another human again and I will hold to that oath. It is the only thing saving me from certain disaster.

My head turns, almost involuntarily, and my eyes sidle back to Pellia on her horse. She looks tired, with dark circles under her eyes. But something about her bearing makes her still appealing. Pellia has only ever been kind to me, light and flirtatious. Is it unfair to her to see Lucy in her image? Perhaps.

But Lucy was beautiful and bubbly when she wanted something. Bewitching enough that I was blind to her flaws. She used me and my clan until she ultimately robbed us. I haven't yet seen flaws in Pellia, but it does not mean they are not there.

We ride for another few hours without incident until we

reach the first affected southern town, Aquilar. The smell of burnt fields greets us as we approach. The surrounding farms have all been affected. Charred black earth surrounds us, as far as the eye can see. The town is quiet, no one on the streets. It's like the inhabitants are hiding from us as we ride up.

Bronwyn rides up beside me and says, "As you can see, the situation is as dire as we said."

Pellia comes forward as well, nodding, "I believed you when you said that the food stores are being attacked, but it is sobering to see it in person. Is there anywhere that hasn't been affected?

The peasant woman shakes her head. "Not in Aquilar. The arsonists attacked for a week, every night a new field being burned, a new farmhouse succumbing to the flame. At first, we thought it was some madman targeting our town, but then the next week, more villages were attacked. Despite that, this town has had it the worst."

"Then, there must be something special about Aquilar," reasons Pellia. "Why were they attacked first and the longest? We need to investigate."

"I will send my orcs to the fields, to see if there is anything that was missed by the magistrate's men," I say. "We should meet with the magistrate while we are here."

"That will be difficult," Bronwyn returns grimly. "He was killed in the last fire while trying to douse the flames in his own fields."

Pellia looks alarmed. "You did not say that there have been deaths because of the fires."

"There have been a few," replies the peasant leader. "Mostly from those fighting the flames. Death does not seem to be their initial goal, as the homes that have been targeted haven't had their exits tampered with, but death has come nonetheless."

"Then who will we speak to?"

"That'll be me," Bronwyn says. "My father was the magistrate and, without a new one being appointed, people have turned to me in the meantime."

The woman is an acting magistrate? No wonder the

common folk at the palace gates had looked to her as leader. Still, the fact that she hadn't shared this previously is suspicious to me.

"Why is this the first we are hearing of this?" I demand, my eyes narrowing at the human woman.

"When would I have told you? When you were intimidating my people at the gate or when you were interrogating me in the Council Chamber? You never asked. And what did it matter? You were going to come investigate without me trying to throw around non-existent titles and demands!"

"Still," Pellia says, gently, her tone obviously trying to calm the argument brewing between Bronwyn and me, "You should have told us. I understand you are doing your best to protect your people, and probably thought that if you told us you had no official authority that we might not listen to you, but secrets in the future will not serve us."

"Noted, Regent," Bronwyn says with narrowed eyes.

The beautiful regent beside me tilts her head and continues, "Did you not think of the fact that we could actually appoint you as the actual magistrate? Make your authority real?"

Bronwyn looks mulish. "I considered it, but I am a young, unmarried woman. Not the type that royals put in charge."

"Not the type that royals put in charge *in the past*," corrects Pellia. "But that was when Adrik was ruled by a human king. Our new orc king is less interested in a person's gender than he is in whether someone can do their job. Is that not so, Warchief Verrick?"

I nod, still glaring at Bronwyn. Something about her stories and excuses I still don't trust. It is difficult to say, however, if it is because her story truly matches up or if it is because she is a human woman. The specter of Lucy hangs over my head again.

"Take us to where we might talk," Pellia says. "Then we can make plans as to what would be best for the south and strategize how we can catch the arsonists."

Bronwyn's lips twist slightly, but nods, "Of course. This way, Regents."

❊ ❊ ❊

Much later, Pellia and I are in my tent once again. Though we were in town much of the day, there was no place for us to sleep. Buildings are a scarce commodity and the inn is full of those whose homes have gone down in the fires. It was a simple thing to have our tents set up in one of the burned fields, close to Bronwyn's home, though the acrid smell of the charred harvest lingers unpleasantly in the air.

Pellia entered my tent again as if she belonged in it and is presently doing her nightly rituals, once again rubbing a sweet smelling oil into her skin, her hair already up in its silken wrap. I'll admit that even in the scant two days that we have been traveling, I am getting used to her presence. Having her close soothes something in me that is restless when she is out of sight.

Finishing her routine, Pellia turns and smiles at me. I wish she would stop doing that and yet I know I would miss her happiness if it was gone.

"You know," she says, "If we are to be lovers, perhaps we should try doing things the Orikesh way."

"What do you mean?" I ask, ignoring the way my heart seemed to skip a beat when she said "lovers."

"Should you not, I don't know . . . thrum? Isn't that what it is called?"

I am taken aback. "How do you know about thrumming? About *sibilance*?"

"We had a demonstration," she replies in the easy way of hers, as if she has no cares. "Before the king and queen's Bride Chase. It was quite thrilling. I enjoyed it immensely, and they said it was something the orcs did during the courting stages of a relationship. So shouldn't you do it now?"

She doesn't say that we are only trying to look as though we are courting, but I suppose we cannot trust where there might not be ears to listen to us. But she is mistaken in her assumptions, or at the very least, it was not explained to her well.

"Thrumming is not for courting," I say bluntly. "It is for seduction."

She steps close to me, a hand coming up to the bracers on my arm, touching me lightly, "And do you not wish to seduce me?"

"Why do you need to be seduced when we are already lovers?" I prevaricate. I do not tell her that, because of my siren mother's heritage, my *sibilance* is stronger than most. If I thrum, we almost certainly would fuck. Or at least she would beg me to do so.

Her hand trails up my forearm to my bicep, a teasing touch leaving fire in its wake. "Every woman wants to be seduced," she says, a slight smile playing at her lips, even as her eyes tell me she is earnest. "Perhaps I want to fully experience what it is like to have you in my bed, Verrick."

She looks up, and I read in her gaze a wealth of promise. She is being serious, and this is a serious offer. Pellia bites her plump lip and waits for my answer, something like hope shining in her eyes.

This is the most bold she has been with me. There was our exchange by the river this morning and she has flirted a few times, but never has she been so open. But I knew that this is what she wanted. Even before we played at lovers, she has always shot sly glances and winks my way, her eyes full of approval for my form.

So the little human wishes to be seduced? Part of me longs to fulfill her desire, to drag her into my bed without pretense and take her in as many ways as our bodies will allow. To thrum in the ways of my father with the strength of voice given to me by my mother. I know that our fucking would be exquisite. But her small hand on my arm reminds me of another's hand. Another time. Another woman.

Lucy, who taught me that fragile, beautiful human women are not to be trusted. That smiles can hide a wealth of lies.

So instead I step back and say, "That would be a bad idea,

Regent Santir."

For a moment, I think I see a shard of hurt in her eyes, but it is quickly replaced with a teasing grin, "Are not bad ideas the most fun?"

"No," I reply firmly. "They are the ideas that lead to the most destruction."

"Huh," she steps back, an assessing look in her eyes, even as a smile still plays at her lips. Then she whispers conspiratorially, "I have never had to actually convince a male to join me in my bed. You are a challenge."

"I assure you, I am not," I say back softly, cognizant that there may be listening ears. "You would do well to find someone else to warm you. Our current arrangement must stay what it is."

And I will try not to kill the other male when her smiles stray from me and land on another, I think.

"Ah, but I do not give up easily," she replies quietly with a touch of teasing in her voice. Then her voice raises to regular volume. "But for tonight I am tired and will leave you be. For *tonight.*"

With that, she swishes away to behind the flap that separates her half of the tent from mine. Her ample hips sway as she walks away and I am a tortured orc. I'm being offered a night or maybe more in the bed of one of the most beautiful women I have ever seen and I am turning it down. Am I a fool? Perhaps we could be casual lovers. Pellia has not shown she wants more than my body. Perhaps it would work.

But even as I think about it, I know I am lying. If I give it any fuel, my Mating Instinct will rise again. It will tell me to take and to Claim. Such tempting fuel is Pellia, with her curves and softness, her dark eyes and long braids of black hair. If I have her even once, I will want to keep her, and keep her I cannot. How can I, when I know I can't trust her?

That thought sits sourly in my stomach. It seems unfair, somehow. Though I know she is a skilled politician, I can't help but think that she has been nothing but open with me, all her actions in line with her words. Not only that, but she has been open with me about secrets, confided in me about the Cabal contacting her, things she did not have to.

But then I think of Lucy, and my heart hardens.

I've been burned once. I'll be thrice-damned before I'm burned again.

CHAPTER 9

Pellia

When I wake in the morning, Verrick is gone again and I find myself annoyed by that fact. I let it be known that I want him in my bed, and then he rejects and avoids me. Did I read him so wrong? Did I overestimate my own charms?

It seems unlikely. I've seen how often his eyes seem to stray to me, even against his own will. I've seen his pupils dilate with passion and the way his body leans towards mine when we are alone.

There is something else at work here. Some offense I've done that I am not aware of, or something in his past that is keeping him from me. I frown. Maybe he has a past love he is staying true to or a forbidden love that is out of his reach.

I don't like those thoughts, but they plague me as I get dressed. What do I actually know about the stern Warchief that I want in my bed? That he is magnetic? To be sure. That he is honorable and serious? Of course. But nothing of his past. I know that there is no one in his life romantically, though. That same honor I've seen would not allow him to bask in my flirtations while going home to another.

No, if there is something keeping him from being my lover, it is something in his past. It irks me that I do not know what it is and I also know that he will not share it with me. Not with his feelings so carefully hidden behind the stone walls of his face.

But these thoughts are not constructive, and I try to banish them as I begin my day. I set up a headquarters at Bronwyn's house, and spend the time giving out food supplies that I have brought from the capital to those that are most in need in Aquilar.

It's certainly not enough, especially since we must keep some of the stores for the other towns we will visit. What will we do when winter is truly upon us all? I'll need to write to Adalind and ask posthaste. I'll also have to tell the Council of Thirteen that the west and north will have to pay the bulk of the tribute to Orik this time around. *That should be fun*, I think sarcastically.

The sun is low in the sky, the evening meal passed, when an orc comes up to me as I fill my umpteenth basket with food and supplies.

"Regent Santir," the orc says, tone grim, "The investigators have returned from the farthest farm and have things they need to relay. Warchief Verrick requests your presence in his tent."

His tent, eh? With all my things in there, it is still *his* tent? I find myself slightly annoyed again. In everything he does, Verrick seems to push me away, even in the choice of his words.

Outwardly, though, I give the orc a smile and put down my basket. "Very well. Have Bronwyn Cooper and her associates been called as well?"

"Yes," replies the orc. "They are on their way now. If you would follow me."

I know where the blasted tent is, of course, but I let the orc lead me. He is merely doing his job.

As I enter the tent, it first strikes me that the flimsy partition blanket that Verrick hangs at night is gone and they have moved my things to one side. The bed is in plain view and, for all intents and purposes, it appears as if we are living together in this tent. I soften slightly. *He is, at least, following the plan*, I muse.

A table with chairs has been placed in the center of the tent.

Verrick sits on the far side of the table, the chair to his right empty, while the others are filled with Bronwyn and her two shadows, Quill and Owen. It appears I am the last to arrive.

I paste a smile on my face and sweep into the tent, saying, "Forgive me if I am late, everyone. I was unaware we were meeting."

I walk to the empty chair, trailing my fingers first along the back of Verrick's seat flirtatiously. The movement does not go unnoticed, as I see the brows of the other humans go up. Good. Hopefully, their tongues will go a-wagging and the tale will spread that the Regent Pellia is seducing the orc Verrick. If it hasn't already from my previous antics. Then the tale will go back to the Cabal and they will think I am doing what they commanded. Perhaps they may even contact me again, to give me further commands, and I will learn more about them and their network. Maybe even the identity of the mysterious "Sting" himself.

For his part, Verrick tenses then relaxes under my barely-there touch. I am once again plagued with the thought that he might not want me. However, though I am bothered by the thought that my pursuit may not be welcome, my smile stays the same as I finally take my seat.

"You are fine," the Warchief responds. "The scouts have just returned and are going to show us what they have found."

He nods to a small contingent of orcs that are standing at attention in one corner. At the nod, the first orc in the line comes forward, a small bundle in his hands.

"We found more 'evidence' of orcs, my chief," says the orc scout, his face grim. "Broken bits of orc-make blades and even the corner of a war banner that were missed by the human watch during their first investigation. They were hidden a little too well, so they were not found with the others. The point is obviously to point the finger in our direction."

"Goodness," I say, looking over the wealth of items the orc has spread across the table. "Where are they finding all this?"

"My guess would be Fort Attis," replies Verrick, looking over the items himself. "The piece of warbanner clinches it for me. If we were doing covert operations, we would not be carrying a banner. That's stupid. But there were many at Fort Attis and the siege there lasted several months. Plenty of time for little pieces like this to fall forgotten to the wayside. Someone has been harvesting pieces from the battlefield, then leaving them here to be found by the humans."

Bronwyn shakes her head, her riot of red curls going wild with the movement. "Of course. Why didn't we think of that?"

"Because you were angry and frightened," I respond, not unkindly. "That makes people easy to manipulate. Likely, you were meant to start rioting and causing problems. It is a testament to your character that you sought to talk first, rather than just move to attacking the orcs."

"Like attacking orcs would have gone in our favor," grumbles Quill.

It is hard to like the man when he is so open with his prejudices. I suppose I can only be grateful that it is Bronwyn, rude as she is, that is in charge, not Quill, who so obviously looks at the orcs with such disdain.

I comment, "No, it wouldn't have. The orcs would have quelled the riots easily, but not without loss of life, which would have stirred up more rebellious sentiment. And the cycle would continue."

"Who would do this?" asks Bronwyn, frustrated. "Who has anything to gain through a revolt?"

The Cabal is the obvious answer, but I do not say it. I'm supposed to be on their side and sharing their existence with Bronwyn and her associates would look suspicious on my part. So instead I reply in an amiable tone of voice, "Adrik and Orik have their share of enemies that would benefit from destabilizing the country. Barakrin to the east has never been our friend and Terria across the sea has long been envious of our trade and wealth. Either of them could have sent agents to light the fires and frame the orcs."

The other humans shudder at the mention of Barakrin,

the shadowy country that is home to dark denizens and ruled by vampires. Though we have never fought openly with our neighbor, many of our people are terrified of them, maybe even more so than they were of the orcs to the south.

Quill shakes his malaise off sooner than the others and asks, "But wouldn't we have recognized strangers in the villages before they could cause trouble?"

"Not necessarily," Owen pipes up, surprising me. "Southern refugees have been going in caravans back home, passing through towns on their way. Anyone from those caravans could have set the fires, then left with their caravans the next day, none the wiser."

"Let's not forget about greed, either," says Verrick, his brows furrowed deeper than usual. "Some of your friends and neighbors could have taken bribes to set the fires as well. Anyone could have been turned."

I wince. That comment is inflammatory, and I can already see the outrage on the other humans' faces. Bronwyn opens her mouth, fire in her eyes and anger in bearing, most likely to refute the statement, but I break in, my tone conciliatory, "We mean no disrespect toward your loved ones. But times have been desperate and foreign spies would be masters of exploitation. There could have been someone that felt they had no choice but to accept a bribe."

"Then what do you expect us to do?" Quill snaps. "You've just told us that anyone could be the perpetrator. We've narrowed down no one and now must suspect everyone."

"Not true," I say. "We've ruled out the orcs."

"Great," the man replies sarcastically, "our overlords are safe. It would have been much easier if it were an orc. At least we would have known them by sight!"

Oh, odious, odious man. I open my mouth, ready to give him a tongue lashing, when Bronwyn surprises me by saying, "Shut up, Quill. You're insulting both the regents and they are the ones trying to help us. Making wishes that our task was easier helps no one."

The redhead looks around the tent and sighs, "Maybe we should take a break and reconvene tomorrow. Tempers are rising, and I doubt we will be constructive."

Verrick nods, "Alright, we will spend another day in Aquilar, continuing our investigation. My orcs will start interviewing witnesses. Then we will move on to Kingsbury. We can't stay here forever."

Agreement echoes through the tent, and one by one everyone leaves until Verrick and I are alone. With a sigh, I lower myself into a chair, my frustration rising.

"He is right about one thing," I say. "It will not be easy to find the individuals serving the greater whole, even if we are sure about the ultimate perpetrator."

The big orc looks thoughtfully at the tent flap where everyone left. "Perhaps," he responds. "But I am starting to have a theory."

"Oh? Do share."

He shakes his head. "Not yet. I want to be sure before I speak things aloud. One can never be too sure who might be listening."

A reminder of the Cabal. They need to believe that I am following their plan and luring Verrick to Grimblton to be slaughtered. If they get any sign that I am playing them, who knows how their plans may evolve or even accelerate? Still, I wish we could speak freely, at least when we are alone. A silence totem would be useful. *Oh well.*

"Alright," I reply. "Keep your own council for now. Shall we go to bed?" I give him a loaded look, one that reminds him we are meant to be playing at lovers.

"Of course," he replies, kind of stiffly. "Let me douse the lumen crystals."

"You can keep them on," I tease lightly, rising and walking toward the bed, a little sashay in my hips. "I don't mind."

"I can see you perfectly in the darkness," he says, snuffing out a crystal. "We do not need to risk others seeing your silhouette outside."

"Can you?" I ask, intrigued. "Are all orcs so gifted?"

Verrick shakes his head. "Orcs can see better in the dark than humans, but my eyes are made for darkness deeper than a moonlit night."

"From your non-orc parent?" I query.

He gives a curt nod.

"How fascinating. Who could have given you such dark-seeing eyes? Are the ogres of Perith your kin?" I ask innocently. "You are so big, after all."

As he moves through the tent dousing lumen crystals, Verrick snorts, "Not likely."

"But you have no markings of troll, nymph, or elf," I reason. "And you seem too big to be of human-get, though I suppose that would explain your dislike of us."

He glances up, his darks unreadable. "I do not dislike humans."

I laugh at that. "Yes, you do."

Verrick grimaces slightly, then goes back to dousing crystals. "I do not dislike all of them."

Hmm. What could he mean by that? Ignoring his vague statement for now, I say, "Then what are your origins?" I ask. "Or am I being too rude? I am merely curious."

He chuckles lightly and says, "I do not mind you asking. But it would be rude, yes, in mixed company. I imagine it would be similar to someone asking you why your skin color is different from other Adrikians."

"Oh," I feel my cheeks heat. I fielded many questions like that as a child and still get discourteous stares sometimes. Having a Sheaothan mother, even one who was princess in her own country, makes me an oddity among the nobles. "I did not mean to make you uncomfortable."

At the last crystal, he stops, then leans back and stretches, his muscles moving in a hypnotic way that makes my mouth go dry. He says, "Come, feel here," gesturing to the tattoo that stretches from shoulder to shoulder over his pectorals.

I step forward, feeling the moment charge with an intimate energy. It is the first time that he has invited me to touch him, I am not unaware of that fact. The act feels heavy with meaning.

Hesitantly, I smooth my fingertips over the ink of his tattoos. Surprisingly, I meet a rough texture. My eyes fly up to his.

"Scales?" I ask.

Verrick nods. "Yes. My father was an orc, but my mother was a siren."

I shudder. Sirens are huge, bigger than the average humanoid, and dangerous. They often lure travelers to their deaths for sport.

"No wonder you can see in the dark, since sirens must see in the deep ocean. But your father was either very brave or very foolish," I say, stroking my fingers along his tattoos again. The texture is mesmerizing. I yearn to reach and feel the rest of his skin, beyond these patches of scales, but I do not dare. He hasn't invited further touch.

"He was both. Perhaps more obsessed than foolish though," he replies, his hand coming up and capturing mine, staying my movement. But now we are holding hands. The warmth from his grasp travels up my arm and into my body, where I feel myself prime for his touch. If only he were not so stubborn.

"Obsessed?" I ask, a little breathlessly, resisting the urge to squirm. He's still holding my hand.

"My father saw my mother on a voyage and leapt over the side of the ship to find her. She didn't want an ugly orc and tried to kill him instead. They struggled for hours, my father never giving up. Orcs are stronger than most and hold their breath for long periods of time, so her efforts to drown him were unsuccessful. Eventually, they landed on a small island and, rather than continue the struggle, my mother abandoned him there. But he camped on the beach for months before she came back. She was surprised that he had waited for her. Most mortals die or escape sirens. Very few actually continue their pursuit. But my father did. They started a strange and fast courtship, then she disappeared again. Three months later, he saw her for the last time, when she came, handed him a baby, and left without a word. He waited for a year after that before returning to Orik, but she never came back."

"How terrible for him," I murmur, "To want her so much and be treated as so disposable."

Verrick merely shrugs. "It is not much different from other races. No one wants an orc."

"That," I say sternly, "is simply not true. What about King Rognar and Queen Adalind? They are true mates now."

"Exceptions exist to every rule."

"Well," I say, summoning up my courage, "What about me?"

This makes him look startled. He looks down and seemingly notices for the first that he is still holding my hand, but still doesn't release it. Then he takes my gaze with his own and says, "You do not know what you are asking for."

"Yes, I do," I retort, "I asked last night, and I will ask again. I want *you.* In my bed, satisfying each other's appetites, with no pretense. It's quite simple."

He leans down close, his eyes still on me, leaning in so that our breath is mingling. Mine hitches for a moment and my core clenches.

"If we were in each other's beds, little one, nothing would be simple."

Oh. *Oh.* I feel myself becoming wet at his words. That squirmy, eager feeling lights low in my belly and I tilt my head slightly, a brazen invitation.

"Show me."

A moment passes. Then two. Just when I think he will turn away, his lips are suddenly on mine, and a deep hunger roars to life. His hands are suddenly around me, pulling me close and mine are around him, yearning, greedy things pulling at his clothes, finding his hair, stroking and touching.

With no effort, he lifts me, pulling me closer, a hand lifting me up under my buttocks, splitting my legs so that my core finds his hardness. I wrap my legs around him, determined to grind against him, when I am suddenly falling through the air, landing on the mattress with a *whump* and Verrick is across the tent, breathing hard in the dim light.

"Wha—?"

"No!" he harshly breathes. "No, temptress. I swore I would keep away from you and I will. Do not do that again."

"But, Verrick, I don't—"

My words land on deaf ears as he tears from the tent like the hounds of the Nether were behind him, and I am suddenly left alone.

What in the world?

CHAPTER 10

Agony

"**M**y lord," says Ache, entering the ritual chamber. "Another falcon has arrived with the message from Sting."

I pause my efforts, the runes drawn in the blood of my victims standing in stark relief on the stones. They tortured the last innocent to death the night previous, and she bled overnight so that her blood could be used in the preparations. It is tedious, finicky work to draw out the runes and I must work quickly, while the blood is still fresh and wet. Would that I could command someone else to do it, but the ritual insists that it must be me, so draw I do.

"Give it here," I command, standing up and taking the scroll from my subordinate. I break the wax seal and quickly peruse the note.

They are on the move. In Aquilar now, in point of fact. The orc is conducting his investigations, none the wiser that he is being led right into our trap. Our agent reports Pellia is doing exactly what we asked her to, seducing the orc and leading him this way and that. Good. I will reward her faithful service and her sacrifice of taking the orc under her skirts.

I find that I cannot wait anymore. Preparations for the ritual are nearly complete here and the boredom is getting to me. The anticipation is too much and I have never been good at depriving myself of anything.

"Send a reply," I order Ache, kneeling back down to finish my work, "When they get to Kingsbury have them greeted in an . . . explosive way. The orc needs something to do with his investigation."

Ache bows and leaves the room. I pick up my brush and dip it in the crimson fluid. I'll finish here and then ride out for Kingsbury.

Perhaps it is time to tell an old friend "Hello."

CHAPTER 11

Verrick

That was too close. Too tempting. Too everything. How can I keep my distance when she offers herself up like that, with a smile and heat in her eyes?

I tear through the encampment, all the way to where the watch stands ready. My orcs look surprised to see me scrambling to place their fists over their chests.

"Warchief..."

"You are dismissed," I say sharply. "I will take this watch."

The scouts know better than to argue with me, merely nodding and clapping their fists to their chests again before leaving. And I am alone. Good.

What was I thinking? We are meant to play the parts of lovers, but never can I actually take Pellia in my arms. Humans cannot be trusted. How often do I need to remind myself of this? Did Lucy not make a most thorough and sadistic teacher?

But for the first time in a very long time, I wanted it. Gods how I wanted it. I wanted her lips and her moans and the sweetness of her cunt. I wanted her on her back and on her knees and every way in between. And I didn't want her because she would be a convenient hole to find relief. I wanted her because she is Pellia. Smiling, beautiful, clever, brave Pellia.

Gods. *Fuck.* I'm in trouble. The Mating Instinct that has been long dormant in me is stirring again. Rumbling awake

like an ancient, powerful beast. How am I to fight it, espe
with my little temptress throwing herself at me? Telling me so
frankly that she wants me? Smelling like a fucking dream? But I
must, because I know that, like all women, when she has gotten
what she wants from me, she will throw me away. Like my
mother did my father. Like Lucy did with me.

So I must resist. I *must*. The only possible ending is pain and
I am not sure that I could survive the blow again, especially at
Pellia's hands.

I stare into the burnt fields, at high alert and resolved to
avoid the tempting little beauty for as long as I can. If I can't then
I will not be able to control my actions, of that I am sure.

Except, we have to play lovers and I can't avoid her. I curse
silently to myself as the moon rises, cresting over the roofs of
Aquilar. How will I keep my sanity staying in the same tent with
Pellia, riding next to her, breathing her same air? My Mating
Instinct growls at me, biting and demanding that I return to my
mate's side, already convinced that I am owned by that small
human, my heart in her delicate hands.

But she is *not* my mate and how can I, when I can't even let
myself trust her? If I let her into my bed, I will let her into my
head and heart as well.

Except already she is in my head, seizing control of all my
waking thoughts, my being turning towards her like a plant to
sunlight. *This has all been a mistake.* This plan must end. I can
follow Pellia into the trap at Grimblton without pretending to be
smitten by her.

I shift in place, knowing that I am lying to myself. I know
I am already smitten. I do not know when exactly it happened,
but it is a disaster, nonetheless.

I must avoid her as much as I can. I don't know how much
longer I resist her charms. Was it not just last night that I
told her that getting involved would be foolish, only to kiss her
merely a day later? She is dangerous.

I have never run from danger, but now I must.

It is the only way.

❋ ❋ ❋

The next day, we interview the citizens of Aquilar before packing up and moving out to Kingsbury, the next big town on our list to tour. As discussed, we will go there next to survey the damage. Our caravan moves slowly, weighed down by the wagons of necessary relief supplies Pellia brought with us.

Still, though I know it is necessary, it makes me antsy. I want to move faster, go through this farce as quickly as I can, and be done with it.

For her part, Pellia chatters happily at my side, as if nothing happened between us last night. Still, her smile does not quite reach her eyes and I feel, for the first time, that she is playing a part around me. I have hurt her with my rejection. She doesn't understand that I am the one broken, that I can never trust her.

I respond only in short answers and grunts, but it doesn't seem to dissuade or stem her cheerful observations. She is determined, it seems, to follow the plan and show the rest of the caravan that we are close and flirtatious. But the longer the day goes with her false cheer and mechanical flirtations, I grow more and more tense. This is not the Pellia I have come to know.

Usually she appears so . . . genuine. *Maybe she is*, whispers a rebellious voice inside me. *Maybe she has been exactly as she appears and you are too stubborn to believe it. Maybe if you allow yourself, you can trust her.*

I barely keep myself from riding away from the caravan, pushing my warbeast to his fastest speed to escape this hell. Pellia's insistence at stopping in each of the smaller villages further slows our pace. We take stock of their damages and pass out food and blankets.

I tersely order my orcs to help, so that these charitable efforts go faster, so that we will arrive at our destination sooner. I hang back and watch, doing nothing to change the glower on my face. My patience is being tested to its limits.

Pellia either doesn't notice my foul temper or doesn't care

about it. Whenever we stop, her genuine smile is back on her face as she listens to each person's needs and gives them what we can. I am orc enough to admit that seeing her real smile focused on others after a day of false happiness focused on *me* nettles even more.

Finally, late in the evening, we arrive at Kingsbury. It is nowhere near as bad as Aquilar, but the countryside is still dotted with burnt fields and houses, a sight that is already becoming commonplace in our travels. We get to the town proper and are greeted by the Kingsbury's magistrate.

"Welcome," the man says, his words less than sincere as he stares at me and my orcs with pointed suspicion. "I am Kade, the magistrate. We are happy to receive a delegation from the capital to put an end to these fires."

"That is why we are here," Pellia returns, cheerfully, addressing the human as if he had been genuine. "We also bring aid for those that were affected most by the fires and food for whoever needs it, since the harvest has not been what it should have been."

The human man perks up slightly at the mention of aid, his eyes passing over the wagons behind us with a sort of desperate light. "That will be most welcome," Kade replies, sounding more unfeigned in his sentiments. "Some that have lost their farms barely have enough food to last through the week, let alone the winter."

Pellia goes to respond to the man again, but at that moment the wind changes direction and the acrid smell of smoke greets my nostrils.

"There is a fire," I announce, my orcs around me tensing at the same time I do.

The beautiful regent to my right looks startled. "A fire? But I don't see smoke. Is—?"

A bell clangs in the distance, an alarm. Shouts of "Fire!" float toward us on the breeze.

Sure enough, soon there is a large, dark billow of smoke in the air, coming from the other side of town.

I bark an order and my orcs move, grabbing blankets from the wagons and then moving with all the speed our orc strength grants us toward the fire.

"Get our mage and the one that was assigned here!" I shout, then spur my warbeast forward into a run, heading in the direction I am led with my eyes and nose.

I am soon greeted by a fast-spreading fire, faster than is natural. Magic? Or some other mischief? Some other smell greets me under the smell of the smoke, though I cannot place it. I leap down from my warbeast, pull the heavy cloak I wear from my shoulders and begin beating in at the flames, attempting to smother them. Other orcs appear at my side, working with the blankets to smother the blaze.

To my left, I can see that the humans have formed a long line of bodies. They are desperately passing buckets of water from the town well to the field, throwing bucket after bucket on the growing fire.

It is useless. The fire moves like a thing possessed, consuming everything in its path. Even with all our efforts combined, this field of grain is going to be lost.

"Where are the mages?" I demand, desperately beating at the flames. If this fire is magical, we'll be lost without our own magical interference.

"Here, my lord!" I hear the yelled response and an older human male scurries next to me, accompanied by a younger man. Air moves unnaturally around them and I glean that their Aspects must be air. Pity that. Water would be more useful.

"Do you sense a magical source to this fire?" I demand, rounding on the older mage. He is smaller than I am, his shoulders hunched as if he were more used to pouring over ancient tomes than being out in the real world.

"Yes!" he says, yelling over the din. "There's a spark of magic in the air, something alchemical feeding the flames. Heinrich and I can try to pull the air away from the blaze and starve the fire, but if we are to stop it, it must be contained. Otherwise, our magic won't be able to work fast enough to douse the inferno!"

Throwing my cloak down, I shout to my orcs, "Find shovels and run to the edge of the field! We have to dig a fire break so that the next field doesn't catch! Hurry, we must contain it for the mages!"

My orcs scramble to follow my orders while I run around the blaze, smoke tearing at my lungs as I breathe. *Was this on purpose?* I wonder. *Did the perpetrators light the fields just as we arrived as a message? A warning? Or to make us look guilty?*

I cannot say, but I don't have time to think. I reach the fence line, just as some of my orcs appear, shovels, hoes, and other tools in hand. One hands me a digging implement and we begin our race against time. The fire is headed this way, tearing through the wheat and headed to the next field.

I don't know how much time passes. The sky is dark by the time we finish, but the fire break works. The trench stops the fire from spreading and the mages pull at the wind, making it lose fuel. It grows smaller, more manageable. The blankets and water can finally do their work. The flames are finally out when the moon is high in the sky, but it is a success. Only one field was lost, the farmhouse and surrounding area protected by the efforts of my orcs.

I turn to the older mage who breathes heavily, obviously tired out by his efforts. "Your plan worked," I say. "My thanks . . ." I realize I don't know his name.

"Hoggins, my lord," the mage supplies, getting my meaning. "My name is Hoggins. I am the Royal Mage, and head of the Mage's Tower. And this is Heinrich, the mage you assigned to Kingsbury. I am pleased we could help these people. And without your orcs, it would have been much worse. My plan wouldn't have worked without your efforts."

I grunt in reply, acknowledging his words, but too tired to keep conversing. My lungs burn with smoke inhalation and my muscles protest my movement. I walk over and reach down to retrieve my cloak, which is completely ruined. With it in my hands, I trudge back to the caravan.

More than one human comes forward to thank me as I

walk, their eyes shining out from soot-stained faces. I know I must not look any better and I yearn to bathe, but our camp is not set up and we must do more work before my orcs and I can rest.

I am surprised, however, when returning to the caravan to see our tents are already raised. The humans we brought with us from the capital are setting them up and cooking enormous pots of stew. They are filling the bowls of many who are lined up to eat.

I catch one human bustling about and ask. "What is all this? How are the tents up?"

The human looks startled to be addressed, but answers, "It was Regent Santir. When she saw the fields were taken care of, she ordered the rest of us to prepare for your return. She said that you would all need respite when you were done and that the rest of the town could use feeding."

Pellia. At the mere mention of her, my Mating Instinct raises its head again, desperate to find her. As I look around the camp, I am reminded that Lucy never did anything like this for me. She never seemed to care about my wants or needs. My comfort.

Because Pellia is not Lucy, my traitorous brain whispers. *She's never been anything like her.*

Banishing my yearning thoughts, I make my way to my tent. I brace myself before entering, expecting a flirtatious human to greet me, but the tent is empty, with the lumen crystals lit and a tub of hot water in the center of the room.

Again, the consideration of Pellia touches me, though I do not want to be softened toward her. My heart is dangerously soft toward her already. Fortifying myself against the gesture, I take a quick bath, eyes constantly glancing toward the tent flaps, waiting for the little human to appear. Do I want her to walk in on me bathing, like she did those scant days ago? *No, of course not*, I chide myself, all the while knowing that I am lying.

I finish my bath and no Pellia. I dress and still no Pellia. Finally, I poke my head out of the tent and see that the bustle of the camp has quieted, my orcs already sleeping or going on watch now that their bellies are full.

I see my second-in-command Friza walking to her watch post, and signal her to come over. She lightly jogs toward me and says, "Warchief?"

"Where is the human regent?"

Friza grins at the question. "That little morsel? Why do you want to know?"

"Just tell me, Friza," I command irritably. My Mating Instinct paces in my chest, not liking that Pellia is somewhere out of my reach.

"She bedded down a while ago with the human servants. She said that you would be tired, and that she didn't want to disturb you."

She's sleeping somewhere else? Oh, my Mating Instinct doesn't like that at all. A growl escapes my chest and Friza's eyes open wide.

"I knew it! You're doing more than pretending to fuck the human. She's your—"

"She's nothing," I lie, my eyes narrowing. I surreptitiously sniff the wind, but I can't smell Pellia at all. She'll have drunk *orikiri* leaf tea in the mornings like an orc, so her scent is muted, only strong emotions discernable. I know that is her habit, one that the queen taught her. I feel the impulse to go tearing through the camp to go find her and bring her back to where she belongs, but I stop myself.

Where she belongs? I'm the one that has pushed her away. For all her excuses that she told others, I know why she is avoiding my bed. There is no one at fault but me. And that is the way things have to be.

"You are dismissed, Friza," I snap.

"Am I?" she says mildly, not moving or leaving to go to her post.

"I don't want to discuss this any further. Especially not right outside my fucking tent."

"Then invite me in, Warchief," Friza returns. "For though

you do not want to discuss it, discuss it we shall."

As my second-in-command, Friza has a lot more latitude in addressing me than anyone else in my clan. Her expression is calm but serious, her body language immovable. If I try to leave this conversation, she'll follow me anyway.

"Fine" I grimace irritably. "Come in, then."

Friza follows me into the tent, the flap closing behind her. We are alone in the tent, but Pellia's scent buzzes around us, an echo of her once-presence here.

The smell makes me more irritable, as it just reminds me that little human is elsewhere. "Say what you have to say and be quick about it," I order Friza.

The orcress looks at me intently, then sighs. "Look, Warchief, when you first introduced this plan to take the human to your bed, none of us said anything. You've been through a lot and you are long past-due for a lover."

"She's not really my lover. You know that," I point out. After scenting thoroughly outside the tent, I am sure that we are alone, at least for now. Besides, we are speaking in Orikesh. I feel like I can discuss things a little more openly with my second.

"Really?" Friza replies. "You feel nothing for her? No possessiveness? No Mating Instinct?"

I say nothing in response, waiting for my second to make her point. She continues, "You've been alone for so long, with some self-inflicted monkhood, that most of us thought you'd never take another mate again."

That spurs a response out of me. "If she's not my lover, she's certainly not my mate."

"But why?" asks Friza. "Why can't she be? She's kind and brightens the room when she walks in. The rest of our clan likes her well enough."

"She's human," I remind her.

"So?"

"So?" I query, surprised that Friza is making me say this aloud. "Lucy was human, and she was my greatest mistake."

Friza looks unimpressed with my argument. "Lucy was a

lot of things, Warchief, including a thief and a liar. Her being human was the least of what she was. Regent Santir is nothing like her. You should know that."

Do I know that? It's hard to say. She acts nothing like Lucy, it's true. But she's a politician, which means she is skilled at lies and half-truths. Maybe the woman I know is nothing but a mask.

I shake my head. "Humans are too good at smoke and mirrors. There's no way for me to trust her."

Friza looks at me in shock. "If you think so little of her, then why did you agree to take her into your bed and follow her plan in the first place?"

I almost growl at my second-in-command at her words. It's not that I think little of Pellia, it's . . . I don't know what it is. Aloud I say, "It's complicated."

"It's not complicated," the orcress insists. "You're Mating Instinct wakes for her, doesn't it?"

"It woke for Lucy," I remind her.

"Godsdamn Lucy! She's a mistake for which you've been paying penance for years! Are you going to be alone forever because of her? Will you allow her to rob you of your future as well as everything else she took?"

I snarl at Friza, but it's a half-hearted sound. To be honest, her words are making sense. Am I punishing myself for past mistakes by denying myself who I want?

Friza shakes her head again and continues, "It's not the regent that you can't trust. You've already shown that deep down, you trust her. Otherwise, you wouldn't have agreed to her plan, a plan that puts your life at risk. How can you say that you trust her with your life and not your heart? She is a good woman, as far as any of us can tell. It's yourself that you can't trust; you've been focused on your mistakes for so long you've forgotten how to trust your own reason. Stop fighting what's right in front of you before you lose it forever."

My second makes a sign of respect by placing both her fists over her heart and finishes. "I've said all I need to say, Warchief, and must attend to my rounds. But please, consider my words. I meant them with all the love I have for my chief."

And with that, she leaves me alone in the tent, my thoughts whirling.

CHAPTER 12

Pellia

I wake to an empty tent. The servants have already risen. I'm embarrassed to have slept so long, especially since I wasn't the one fighting fires and setting up camp all night. Hastily I rise, only to hear a crinkle sound as I do so. Someone has tucked a piece of paper under my pillow. Curious, I pick it up and read:

Go to the woods

No sooner have I seen the message when the paper crumbles to nothing in my hands and is gone. Dustpaper. It's used to pass clandestine messages and destroys itself once the message is read. There is only one group that I can think of that would send me secret missives.

A shiver runs down my spine. The Cabal is summoning me. But why now?

Quickly, I dress in the clothes I brought with me last night and remove my silk wrap, letting my braids fall free. Hopefully, I haven't made them wait long. If I've annoyed them, it will be hard to get them to take me further into their confidence.

I make my way out of the servant's tent and toward the treeline. Kingsbury is right next to the Dense Wood, an ancient and eldritch forest where fairies and monsters are rumored to dwell. It's not the smartest thing I've ever done to enter the woods by myself, but I need to obey the message. Hopefully, daylight will afford me some safety.

I have not gone far when the thickness of the foliage has cut me entirely off from being visible from the camp. I go to take another step when the air thickens around me, the sounds of the forest fading, the telltale sign of a silence totem being used.

"You're late," comes Sting's voice, though yet again I cannot see him.

"I came as soon as I got your message," I say, my voice a little breathless from my exertions in the forest.

"So I saw," he responds. His voice sounds disembodied and surrounds me. It's impossible to tell which of the giant trees he could be hiding behind. Who is Sting? Is he following our party, or has he integrated himself into the caravan somehow? That thought is disturbing. I picked all the servants we brought with us personally, which would mean that Sting is most likely a trusted palace staff member.

"Will you still not let me see you?" I say, trying to sound petulant and disappointed instead of eager. He sees me as Yorian's spoiled mistress, so that's the part I must play.

"You don't need to see me, you just need to obey me," he replies. The words are so arrogant that it takes a great effort on my part not to roll my eyes at him.

"I'm trying to serve," I say instead, opting for a humble delivery.

"Then why are you failing?" bites back the voice.

This surprises me. "What do you mean? I've done everything you asked and brought everyone to the south."

"Yet you slept apart from the orc last night," comes the voice. How closely are they watching us? And is it just Sting or are there other traitors in our midst?

"He was tired and in a foul mood from the fire," I return, my tone logical. "I thought there was no way to seduce him in such a situation anyway and went to get some proper rest. I'm exhausted from having to keep up this front with the orc."

Not really. But I am tired of Verrick running away from me. So I let that frustration color my tone, making my words sound true.

"That's not what we discussed," Sting says. "You need to keep him distracted until we can take him in Grimblton. He cannot suspect a trap."

He already knows about the trap, idiot, I think cheekily, but aloud I say, "I'm sorry. You're right. I'll renew my efforts tonight."

"You'd better," the shadowy voice threatens, his tone promising cruelty. "If our plan fails because of you, you won't live to regret it."

I shrink, hoping I look sufficiently cowed. Really, I can't help but think what Verrick would do if he caught this coward. Sting fears discovery so much he hides from a defenseless female, yet is arrogant enough to sling around threats. Definitely a coward.

"I know," I respond. "I'll be better, I promise. And I won't get caught."

"You'd best not. We don't leave pawns alive to squeal about our plots if they do."

The air around me ripples, the silence totem being lowered and I instinctively know I'm alone again, the illusive Cabal member having slithered off after issuing his warning.

What am I to do? Verrick wants nothing to do with me and after I have humiliated myself by throwing myself at him, I don't really want to see him either. But the Cabal is watching us and if we do not play the part of lovers, then they will grow suspicious. Perhaps they will even move when we are not ready for them.

This is all my fault, I know. I tried to mix pleasure with work and it's only gotten me into this fix. I should have kept everything strictly business between us instead of trying to entice the grumpy orc into my bed on top of navigating the Cabal's plot.

I walk out of the woods and run straight into the same orc that was sent to retrieve me last time. He looks surprised, but quickly schools his emotions under an expressionless mask.

"Warchief Verrick requests your presence in his tent. There have been some developments."

Developments? What could that mean? I'm intrigued enough that I almost don't even think about how awkward it will be to see Verrick this morning after I left him alone the night before. I follow the orc to the tent when I realize something.

"You've come to fetch me twice and I still don't know your name," I say to the silent orc as we walk through the encampment. "Will you tell me?"

If he is startled by my addressing him, the orc makes no sign of it. "My name is Korovi ka Roknir, Regent Santir," he replies, still walking with steady movements.

"Ka Roknir?" I ask.

"It's the Orikesh way of surnames," he responds. "The *ka* denotes that we are of a clan, with the following name the name of the clan. So I am Korovi of clan Roknir, Warchief Verrick's clan."

He sounds proud of the fact, and why wouldn't he be? Verrick is a great Warchief from what I have seen and leads a strong and thriving clan.

Hmm . . . Verrick ka Roknir, I think, putting together his full name. It's a good name. Strong, like a fortress wall. I sigh. Must I be attracted to everything about the orc, even his name? It would not be so bad if he wanted me too. I thought for the longest time that he did, thought I could see the longing in his eyes, the slight blush in his ears when he was around me, but I think I was mistaken.

He did *kiss you*, comes the treacherous thought. And then my thoughts are full of that kiss. How desperately he seemed to devour me. How soft his lips were, how he seemed both frenzied and careful, like an amorous worshiper.

My thoughts are still lustful as we enter the tent. Verrick is there, as well as Quill and Bronwyn. Why am I always the last one to arrive? I'm annoyed and so I almost don't notice that Owen is missing, but Bronwyn asks, "Why have you called us here? And where is Owen?"

Verrick acknowledges I am here with a glance from fathomless and unreadable eyes before nodding to one of his orcs.

"Bring the human."

In moments, Owen is dragged in, swearing and struggling, his hands tied in front of him. He sports a black eye. Bronwyn gasps and turns to Verrick, fire in her eyes. "What is the meaning of this? Untie him, now!"

Verrick ignores her commands and instead says, "Tell her, human. Tell her about your treachery."

The human man looks terrified. His eyes dart back and forth between me and Verrick, then desperately at Bronwyn. "I don't know what you are talking about," Owen says, his voice shaking.

"Don't bother with the prevarications," Verrick scoffs, his dark eyes narrowing. "Orcs can smell lies."

This is true. It is why I drink that dreadful tea Adalind gave me every morning, to mute the scent of my feelings from the orcs I am surrounded by.

But the fact is not well known, and Owen grows even more pale at the words.

"Leave him be!" exclaims Quill. "He's not involved. He's been trying to help."

"He is involved and just how involved we will soon see."

"Truly, Regent," Owen says, his voice sounding even more panicked, "I am not lying. I—"

"You are lying now and you were lying two nights ago when you spoke about the perpetrators coming from the refugee caravans. But what clinches your guilt is this."

Verrick pulls out a bottle that looks like a bottle of wine, but as it comes into view, Owen's eyes bug out.

"I've never seen that before. Regent—"

"Stop lying!" shouts the orc Warchief. "We found this among your things. The contents of this bottle reeks of magic and matches the smell of burning fields. Now, we know you weren't the one that lit the fire last night, but I would be willing to bet that all the fires in Aquilar were your doing."

Bronwyn looks shocked, almost like she's going to be ill.

"Owen . . . is this true?"

Desperate, Owen lunges away, only to be caught and pulled back to his seat by Korovi.

"May I?" I say, holding out my hand for the bottle. Verrick passes it over and I undo the stopper. Instantly a strong smell reeks through the air and I put the stopper back.

"Ifrit oil," I declare, looking at Owen with shock.

Murmurs break out in the tent and then Bronwyn's voice breaks through the din. "What is ifrit oil?"

"An alchemical potion, crafted by witches," I explain. "Even a drop can turn the smallest fires into an out-of-control blaze in seconds. It's rare and dangerous to make."

"And how do you know that's what it is?" Quill demands.

"Do not speak to me that way. *I* am not the enemy," I retort, tired of the man's belligerent and constantly disrespectful tone. It's surprising he isn't the traitor. "I know what it is because I have smelled it before. In my mother's homeland it's used to light fires in the desert where there is no kindling. Used correctly, a small amount in a controlled area will burn all night. But if the area is not controlled, like say, a field . . ."

"Then the fire will grow huge and out of control faster than it can be stopped," Verrick finishes grimly, his eyes never leaving Owen, who is glancing around wildly, as if he can still make his escape.

"Where on earth did he get such a thing?" I ask. "It is not as common outside of the deserts of Sheaotha."

"Either he is an agent of Sheaotha," Verrick says, though we both know this is not the case, "or he has contacts that are rich enough to ship something this destructive from across the sea." Ah, much more likely. Sheaotha has trading contracts with many of the nobles of Adrik. The reason my father married my mother in the first place was to procure the first of such contracts from my grandfather, the sultan. It makes sense that one of the Cabal must have such ties as well.

The Warchief steps forward, looming over the human like the death goddess Karnia herself. "Who are you working for?

What is the purpose of these fires?"

Owen's mouth opens and clothes several times, like he is at a loss as to what to do, when Verrick's second in command enters the tent.

"Warchief," she says, "a human has entered camp and demands to see you. He says he is Duke Strand, the lord of these lands."

"Antony is here?" I ask, perplexed.

Verrick just glowers, his eyes never leaving Owen. "Tell him to wait. An interrogation is taking place."

She places her fists over her heart and leaves the tent. All of our attention goes back to the quivering human man before us.

"Owen," Bronwyn says, "just tell them! I know you must have been coerced into this plot if you are involved. Just tell them so that we may save our people!"

Owen opens his mouth, but Verrick snorts, gesturing to one of his orcs who offers a bag. "This was found among his things as well," Verrick says, taking the bag and tossing it to the ground. It bursts open to show it's filled with gold coins, far more than a peasant farmer like Owen could make in a year.

"Don't let him try to say that he did this for any cause other than his own gain. The evidence speaks for itself."

"Please!" pleads Owen, finally speaking up. "I can't tell you. It is impossible! They made me swear a vow . . ."

"Who, Owen?" Bronwyn asks, unshed tears in her eyes, "Who did you make a vow with to sell out your own people?"

"It's not like that! But I can't give you any information. If I try to tell you anything then I—"

Suddenly, the man's voice cuts off and he begins shaking, his eyes rolling into the back of his head. Pink froth spills from his lips and blood trickles from his nose. Bronwyn rears back. "What's happening?"

"Hex!" I exclaim. "Quick, we need a healer! And Hoggins!"

Verrick barks an order, and orcs move to follow our commands, but our reaction seems too late. The human man convulses, falling to the ground, blood pooling under his head.

I dive forward, reaching to right him, to stop his shaking, to do *something*, but powerful arms hold me back.

"No!" snaps Verrick, holding me in his arms, "Do not touch him! The curse could travel to you."

There is nothing to do but watch in abject horror as the man in front of us twitches two more times before going still. A moment later, a healer bursts into the room, wearing a long robe and gloves, but Owen is already gone. Hoggins enters a moment later and gasps when he surveys the scene. Bronwyn begins to weep, her sobs rending the air as Quill holds onto her, stopping her from collapsing on the ground.

The healer examines the body and shakes his head. "This hex is strong, one of the strongest I've ever seen. The body needs to be burned immediately or he'll become one of the undead."

"Can you find the origin of the curse?"

The healer shakes his head. "I am no mage or witch."

"Hoggins?" I ask, looking to the Royal Mage.

The older man crouches down. He takes a handkerchief out of his pocket and uses the fabric to move the dead man's head this way and that, careful not to touch the body with his bare skin. Finally he says, "This is dark magic; witchcraft. I would say that it is a Midnight Oath, something that, if broken, instantly punishes the oathbreaker."

"But he hadn't even said anything! He was only telling us he *couldn't* tell us anything!" sobs Bronwyn. Quill is holding her in his arms as she continues to weep.

"That may or may not be true," Hoggins replies. "We don't know the exact wording of the oath. Maybe even by telling you of the vow, he broke it. But I can tell you that this type of curse can also be triggered remotely by someone with the activating word. So it might have been nothing he said."

"How would they even know to trigger it?" I ask, "How did they know we were interrogating him?"

"There is a spy in our midst," Verrick says grimly. "Someone in the camp must have overheard him and stopped his mouth before he could reveal what he knew. Guards!"

Two orcs come into the tent. "Round up anyone that was around this tent, within fifteen feet. They all need to be interrogated. One of them is a spy for our enemy."

He then turns back to the healer and says, "Gather whatever orcs you need to build a pyre and get this body out of my tent. Now."

There's a flurry of movement as everyone rushes to do what they were ordered. Hoggins and the healer bow, leaving the tent. I turn to Verrick. "Will your orcs really be able to get everyone? What if they didn't see someone?"

"They will get everyone," Verrick says grimly. "They will hunt them by scent."

He then gives me a look I cannot read and says, "You know the human noble that has arrived at the camp?"

"Antony?" I ask confused, "Yes, of course. We were children together and have interacted on the Council of Thirteen. Though he has been ill lately and hasn't been in the most recent sessions."

"Then go and meet him and find out why he is here. I have no time to meet with him. I must settle everything here."

I nod my head. I can do that, and I wish to leave the tent as soon as possible. It smells of blood, even to my weak human nose.

"Very well," I say. "I'll meet with him and bring him to one of the town inns to talk. Come find me, when you are able."

He nods and says, "Take Korovi as your escort. Things have just become very dangerous."

"You can't think that the enemy will target me?" I ask incredulously.

Verrick steps forward, leaning down and speaks quietly into my ear, "You have had dealings with the Cabal as well. If they are feeling threatened, they may start doing away with assets. You need to be careful, Pellia."

His words make me shiver and I remember Sting's threats from a mere hour ago. Was this what he meant? I have made no vows to them, but maybe they have already placed a hex on me, unbeknownst to me.

The thought makes my blood run cold. I nod to Verrick, then to Korovi, before practically fleeing the tent. I need to get away from the reminder of what my fate could be.

Putting that thought behind me, I set out, Korovi on my heels, to find Antony.

But I swear I can feel eyes on me as I go. Verrick's? Or someone more sinister? Shuddering, I banish the thought put on my political face, charm and social graces wrapping me like a familiar cloak. A defense. I'll need it with Antony. Though we have been friends for ages, he's a slippery bastard.

It's fairly easy to find him. He's a tall man, about as tall as one of the shorter orcs, and he dresses in the highest fashions like his station dictates, with a neatly trimmed beard. Ducal arrogance rolls off of him in waves, as he stands in the midst of the camp. When he sees me coming, however, a warm smile breaks over his face.

"Pells!"

I smile in return, the expression a little forced after what I have just witnessed. "Antony! What a surprise to see you here. Are you over your illness?"

"That thing? Just a trifling cold, really. I wanted to join the Council anyway, but my healer nearly had a conniption and forbade me. What can you do? But here I am now and here you are."

He gives me a welcoming bow, his manners as polished as ever. "And I heard that your party saved Kingsbury from a certain doom last night. You have my everlasting thanks."

I laugh. "Always so good with words. Flattery will get you everywhere, you know."

We share a grin and then I grow more serious. "But Antony, why did you not send word about the southern fires to the capital? We had to learn about it from a group of commonfolk that were quite ready to storm the High Citadel in their anger."

The duke before me grows more serious as well. "I am sorry about that. I should have kept a tighter rein on my people. I didn't report it, because I have no information about the perpetrators. The bedrest the healer forced on me has made it hard to run an investigation. It's why I'm so glad you and your party are here, though. This madness must end, especially before winter."

"You are right," I concede, "but let's not speak of it out here. Is there an inn or tavern where we can go to discuss things away from prying eyes?"

"The Fox and Thorn should be quiet this time of day. Shall we go there?"

"Lead the way, Antony."

The duke puts out his arm, and I weave my hand through it. He leads me toward the town, leaving the disturbing death of Owen behind me.

CHAPTER 13

Verrick

The day's interrogations reveal frustratingly little. None of the servants that were outside the tent heard or saw anything and none of them were lying either. Agitated and tired, I decide to seek Pellia. Though I am still in turmoil where she is concerned, I know I will have no peace until I see her again. My Mating Instinct will make sure of that.

Heading into town, I check with my orcs to see where Pellia is. I'm surprised to hear that she is still in the tavern with the human noble. I'm not sure that I like that. Not at all, but I must go to where she is. As I walk, I see several humans look my way as they go about their daily tasks. Unlike Aquilar, where everything we did was met with suspicion and antagonism, I see glances of approval. Even whispers of friendly sentiment. It seems our fighting the fire the night before has done wonders for the orcs' reputation.

Usually I would not care about the opinions of a few paltry humans, but now . . . I see them as Pellia's people. She cares about them and now I find I do too, to a degree. Before, serving them was merely a matter of honor and duty, but now I find myself worrying, as she does, about how they will make it through the winter with fires attacking their fall harvests. Perhaps I should order some of my clan to stay and help bring in the crops. With the superior strength and speed of orcs, it should go faster. The silos will need to be made fireproof, however, as I wouldn't put it past the Cabal to attack those as well once the stores are in.

My meandering thoughts bring me to the tavern where I was told Pellia was and, as I step through the door, I hear a gale of laughter, a genuine sound, coming from the regent's lips. She sits with a human, smiles wreathing her face. The human male looks smug at her laughter, as if very proud of the joke he has told. I am reminded of how unhappy I have made Pellia in the last few days and am instantly jealous that this man has changed all that in the span of a few hours.

I stride across the room, a storm brewing in my mind, when Pellia sees me. Her smile grows a little more wary, and that stops my approach. What am I doing? What right do I have to be jealous? I have pushed Pellia away at every turn and now I want to dictate who she can smile with? It would be laughable if it weren't so wrong.

Instead, I change my approach, coming up more carefully and say, "Regent Santir," in greeting.

Her wary smile stretches a little wider, though it does not quite meet her eyes. I am stung with regret. "Warchief Verrick," she greets in return. "May I present Antony, Duke Strand? His lands encapsulate Aquilar and Kingsbury, the target of most of the attacks."

Hmm, that's interesting. Could he be one target of the attacks? Could the Cabal have some issue with him? I give him a stiff nod, the most respect I can force myself to offer, but he seems to take this in stride, nodding his head a little lower, probably in deference to my title as Orc Regent.

"Warchief Verrick. It is good of you to join us. Pellia tells me that you have been investigating the death of one criminal responsible for the fires. Have you found anything?"

I grunt, but politely reply, "Unhappily, not much. The servants around the tent at the time of the death are innocent. So the perpetrator and whoever is ultimately behind the attacks are still hidden."

The human male frowns. "That is unfortunate news

indeed. What can be done? What can I do to help? I've already sent additional guards into all the towns, but after the war with Orik, my forces are thin."

"This is why we sent the Air and Water mages south and Warchief Verrick has generously brought his orcs. They have been helping where they can and performing their investigations. With their strong senses they have already discovered much that was not known before." Pellia smiles at me on this last sentence, a little more genuinely, before turning the smile back on Duke Strand. I already miss it and long to sweep her away to our tent, where we can be alone. I want to speak to her. I *need* to speak to her.

"That is great news," the human male is saying, replying to Pellia and oblivious to my longing thoughts, "I'm sure with the both of you working on it, the problem will soon be solved."

With that statement, he pushes back from the table and stands, bowing slightly toward Pellia. "Well, it has been lovely catching up with you, Pells, but I must attend to my responsibilities. I must coordinate rebuilding efforts if the people are to be safe. I will leave the investigation efforts in your capable hands."

With that, he bows again, reaching to take Pellia's hand and places a reverent kiss on the back. Instantly, all my protective instincts are roused and my Mating Instinct surges. That is not the action of a platonic friend. They have some sort of past together, or at least the damn human carries hope for a deeper relationship with her in his heart.

Barely keeping back the urge to strike the male for putting his hands on my female, I notice he has given me a truncated sort of bow as well, but can only return it with a curt nod, reigning myself in as I am. Instead, I say to Pellia, "We should go as well. I have some things I need to discuss with you in camp."

Pellia raises a quizzical brow and gives me a befuddled smile, but she rises as well. Without missing a beat, I place my arm out to escort her, a human mannerism. She looks surprised, but takes my arm and I lead her out of the tavern. The beast in my chest quiets now that I have her hand on me, soothed t touch. We probably look odd, an orc play-acting a genteel human and escorting a lady, but I don't care. I just want her close to me.

I lead her through town and straight to our tent. It is in a new spot. Owen's death lingered in the old location, his blood staining the earth. I did not want to risk the curse remaining and affecting Pellia, so I had ordered it moved while I interviewed the servants.

If Pellia is surprised at the tent's new location, she makes no mention of it and merely walks inside with me, the flap closing behind us. When we are alone, she pulls her hand from my arm and wraps her arms around her as if to ward off some chill. She looks small and vulnerable as she asks, "You wanted to say something to me?"

Suddenly, I feel tongue-tied. I do have things I want to say to her. *Everything.* But dare I say them? There will be no returning from this, I know. If I let my Mating Instinct off the leash, it will want to her in all ways. My possessive feelings will only grow.

So, like a coward, I say instead, "You are upset with me."

"Really?" she asks, quirking a brow, a little of her usual teasing self coming through. "And why would I be upset with you? It's not as if I offered to be your lover in truth and you rejected me not once, but twice."

I wince at her gentle admonishment. "I did not mean for them to be rejections."

At that she laughs, the sound not entirely kind. "Did you not? You told me that being with me was a bad idea and then ran from me like I meant you bodily harm! How are those not rejections?"

"Do not laugh like that, I beg you."

"Like what? Like what you are saying is not ridiculous? Like I am not embarrassed and more than a little humiliated?"

"I never meant for you to feel that way. It is not you that is broken. I . . ."

"You think I am not broken?" she asks softly. "Just because I laugh and smile and flirt? You think I cannot feel pain?"

"I did not mean . . ."

But Pellia's words are gaining steam and she plows through my attempt at speech. "I know that there may be many who think that I have never experienced hardship, but I did not know you were one of them."

Disappointment colors her voice.

I am shocked. "I never said . . ."

"You did not need to say so," she retorts hotly. "I can see how you are treating me. But I smile *because* I am broken. Because if I cried and whined and gnashed my teeth every time something terrible had happened in my life, I would get nothing done! I would be stuck in those moments forever. So I defy them instead and I laugh and I flirt because I *want* to, and nothing life throws my way will stop me."

She starts unfastening her dress and I suck in a sharp breath, totally thrown by the unexpected action. But before I can say anything, my eyes grow wide and I see what she is showing me. There, between her perfect breasts, is a gnarled and angry scar; a brand in the shape of the coat of arms.

"This is the brand of House Howser. Yorian's house. Something he gave me the moment I came of age. He wanted to own me in all ways." She tells me, a defiant light in her eyes. She stands proud, showing me this old, hurt, looking for all the world like a wounded goddess, beautiful despite her scars.

"I have lived through terrible things," she tells me, as my jaw clenches tighter the longer I look. "Unimaginable things! I have been hurt and controlled and made to witness all manner of heartache. So do not think me ignorant for enjoying life. I have earned every damned one of my smiles and every tiny moment of happiness. I intend to enjoy every last one of them."

She goes to fix her top, pinning the broaches back in place, when I move with instinct, staying her hand, my large fingers dwarfing her own. I stroke her skin, my black claws sheathed, my fingertips soft. Down they trace, before stopping right above the brand, a question in my eyes.

"It doesn't hurt," she whispers the answer. "Not any longer."

My expression doesn't change, but my heart bleeds for her. How can this bright being of light and laughter have been treated so shamefully? My fingers start moving again with a mind of their own, soothing their way over the old burn. I can tell the skin is still sensitive there, and she shivers a little at the gentle touch. Suddenly I can no longer bear it. My fingers are on her chin, tipping her head back, and then my lips are on hers.

It is a simple thing to kiss Pellia. It feels necessary, as if she were my very breath.

My passion rises and my cock grows hard the longer I am touching her, but my control is iron. I won't kiss the way she might expect a rough and large orc like me would kiss. Instead, my kiss is soft and gentle, punctuated with teasing nips and long, leisurely movements. She gasps against my lips, breathless, and pushing closer to me, and I chafe at the clothes between us. I end the kiss. She stiffens slightly, like she is bracing herself for me to run hot and cold once again, but I am all hot now. Instead, I kiss her cheeks, her nose, her forehead. Reverently, almost, the caresses filled with a leashed sort of need. I want to treat her like she deserves, to worship as I have always wanted until both of us are replete and satisfied.

"I am tired of fighting you, temptress," I sigh into her hair, my arms coming around her body and pulling her even closer. Her bare breasts crush against my chest and I yearn to feel her naked everywhere.

"Then stop," she says simply, leaning forward on the tips of her toes to take my lips again.

"I am not looking for a mate, I . . ."

"I'm not asking to be your mate," she teases, her hands coming to my chest to unbuckle the harness that usually holds my ax. We are both wearing too many things, I decide. "I am asking to be your lover. Not because of any plans but because it is what we both need. Let us stop playing, Verrick, and start living."

I groan at that and take her lips again, this time tinged with le more desperation. There's a more force behind this kiss and she opens to welcome the invasion of my tongue.

Finally.

CHAPTER 14

Pellia

Verrick is kissing me. Kissing me like he's drowning and I am air. Kissing me like we can meld our two forms together with just his masterful lips.

I came into this tent a little angry and shy and uncertain, but I am none of those things anymore. I am a temptress. *His* temptress. I work the buckle of his harness free and slide the straps down his arms, letting my fingers tease his skin as I do so. He kisses me again, my bare top now slides against his, free of any impediment.

He says against my lips, "Do you like this dress?"

"Tear it," I say, throwing caution to the wind, "I don't care. I want to feel you."

He growls and the sound of ripped fabric is in the air, my ruined dress falling to the ground, leaving me only in my underthings. Another rip and I am naked. He makes quick work of his warkilt and then pulls me closer, delicious skin against skin.

He picks me up and my legs instinctually wrap around his torso. I want to feel his malehood against me, but he is too tall and instead I am rubbing against the muscles of his stomach, the ridges teasing my clit and making me grow wet.

"Temptress . . ." he hisses against my mouth, peppering in more light and teasing kisses. Surprising from a man who has always been so taciturn and serious. "You smell so good . . ."

He carries me to the bed and tosses me on the furs. I laugh lightly at the desperate move and then he is on me again.

"But I am sure you will taste even better . . ." he says, sliding down my body, kissing each of my breasts before massaging them with strong, deft hands. He eyes my brand, but before I can feel self-conscious, he gives it a light, gentle kiss, teasing the sensitive skin, before continuing his quest downward.

He is between my thigh before I realize what he means. "You cannot want to . . ."

"I want to," he growls. "I must or I will go insane. Do not tell me no one . . . ?"

"No one," I say, opening my legs wider in blatant invitation. "I've never . . ."

"Well, that is unacceptable," he replies, then buries his face in my center. With the first lick of his tongue, I begin to squirm. With the second I am writhing. Then, he begins to *thrum*. A wash of additional arousal washes over me and I cry out. When he licks me again, I almost scream. His tongue is *vibrating*.

Soon, faster than I ever have in my life, I am coming. But still he thrums and thrums, licking and sucking, pushing fingers into my eager, quivering channel. And I am coming again and again. *This* is the orc's *sibilance*? How are there not women following them, constantly crying and begging to be fucked? I would. I would beg, I am begging. Begging him not to stop. Over and over. I come and I beg and the world melts away into lust and bliss.

Whenever I think it's too much, that I can't possibly come anymore, Verrick thrums again and renews my passion, taking me to higher and higher levels of bliss. I did not know it was possible to feel this good. When he finally pulls away, I am a shivering ball of euphoric nerves.

"You've . . .you've fucked the brains out of me," I say. "I can't even think right now."

He darkly chuckles and replies, "Oh, temptress, that was just the appetizer. Now we have dessert."

He flips me onto my belly and props up my hips. Excitedly, on shaking legs, I open for him, and feel him start to push inside me. He's big. So big, I almost wonder if I can't take him into my small body. But then he begins to thrum again and I choke out a laugh and curse.

"You vibrate here too? Oh, you wonderful, *terrible* orc. I'll never forgive you for not taking me to bed sooner."

"I'll make it up to you," he says, ever serious, and then he pushes all the way inside. I moan. I can't help it. He pushes on everything inside of me and feels so good. I've never been wetter in my life as he pistons his hips, thrumming and vibrating. My blood feels thick and full of arousal, and soon I'm coming again on every thrust. I scream like a banshee, but Verrick only laughs.

"Take me, temptress," he says. "Take all of me!"

Then he roars, coming into my pussy, and I reach my peak again. Then he is collapsing, falling onto the bed, but he pulls me with him, draping me over his heaving chest. I am more satisfied than I have ever been in my life. I drink in great gulps of air, feeling my over-stimulated flesh calm as we lay in silence, breathing together.

Then Verrick starts slightly and says, "I came inside you. I lost control. What if .. ?"

I place fingers on his worrying lips, smiling lazily in the aftermath of pleasure. "Worry not," I raise up my hand, showing him the ring that glints on my right pinky. "I have a contraception charm that I wear here. You are safe to come in me as often as you like."

I do not tell him the reason that I have the charm or why it is worn in such a surreptitious place. That I secretly acquired it when I was with Yorian, that I could not stand the thought of bearing the tyrant king a child, even as I knew Yorian wished for it. It is so small and light that I almost never think about it, wearing it out of habit. But now, at least, I have gotten to use it for my own purposes instead of just in fear.

Banishing the thought of Yorian, I remember what Verrick told me all those nights ago. That orcs have *stamina*.

I reach down with my hand, grip his already-hard cock and barely keep myself from giggling. A hand suddenly spanks my flank and I jump, the blow not hard enough to hurt, but shocking and arousing at the same time.

"Naughty temptress," growls Verrick underneath me, before rolling so that I am under him. "Already so insatiable for your orc?"

I bite my lip and then smile at him. I wrap my legs around him, pulling my womanhood toward his pelvis. "Merely wishing to test your own words, My Warchief. You said orcs can go all night."

He nods, a small smile playing at his normally severe mouth. Apparently, I've fucked the seriousness out of him. For now.

"Show me?" I ask, placing a teasing kiss at the corner of that smile.

And he does.

❀ ❀ ❀

In the wee hours of the morning, I finally call out my surrender. My lust is nothing in the face of an orc's stamina. I've had so many orgasms, I almost thought the pleasure would kill me.

I snuggle into Verrick's side, replete and satisfied. Looking up at his face, I see that small smile on his mouth and smile back, triumphant. We lay in satisfied silence for a moment, a sleepy atmosphere taking hold, but it makes me wonder.

"Why did you push me away before?" I ask, breaking the silence. "Why couldn't we have been here sooner?"

Verrick is silent, his muscles tensing beneath me. I worry that I should not have asked when he finally responds.

"I had a mate before," Verrick murmurs. "A human woman named Lucy."

Now it is my turn to tense. "Did she . . . did she die?" I ask, my heart in my throat. I don't know that I want to compete with the ideal memory of a dead woman.

Verrick surprises me when he snorts. "I hope so. I don't know, though, if she is dead or alive."

I raise my eyebrows. "How could you say such a thing if she was your mate?"

He's silent again, the quiet stretching into awkwardness. For a minute, I think that my new lover won't answer me when he starts telling the story.

"When I first became a Warchief, I was still fairly young. Barely past the point of adulthood, really. One night, not long after I became the leader of my clan, a thief was caught trying to steal the clan treasures. It was a human woman. The sight of her . . . it woke my Mating Instinct."

My breath catches and I feel light-headed listening to his words, but I dare not interrupt. He continues, "Like I said, I was young. Untried. Foolish. I released her from her captivity and offered to make her my mate. She agreed. I thought she was drawn to me at the time as well. Now I know that she just wanted to avoid the punishment for her attempted theft."

He goes quiet again, his gaze far away, and I know he is lost in his memory of this thief. Lucy. I wait with bated breath for the rest of the story, but don't push him to share faster than he is able. Finally, he begins again.

"We were together for a year. I was obsessed with her and did everything I could to make her happy. I showered her with silks and jewels. She was given the best mounts, the best food, the best of everything. Anything she asked for was hers. I expected nothing from her, just her presence. But she never was pleased for long. Nothing was ever good enough. I could never make her happy."

My heart breaks for the strong male beneath me and I begin softly stroking the skin of his chest, silently comforting him, while getting angrier and angrier at this past mate of his. He saved her from the consequences of her own actions and she just kept using him, making him miserable?

He keeps talking. "Though she wasn't satisfied, she had her moments when she would be bubbly and flirtatious. Usually when she wanted something, but still. I thought we would eventually be happy in our own way. And even though it was forbidden during that reign of the last king and I knew I would lose my place as Warchief, I wanted to Claim her, to make her my one and only. But every time she would reject me. She accused me of wanting to put a leash on her and I could never change her mind."

That at least I can understand. Claiming seems so . . . final. So unescapable. I can see why it would scare the other woman. But I keep my thoughts to myself.

Verrick pauses and I can tell this next part is the hardest for him to say. "Then . . . one day . . . I woke up, and she was gone. Her jewels were missing and so was her warbeast. She had left me. But that wasn't the worst . . . my clan treasures were missing too . . . the treasures of my ancestors she had been trying to take in the first place. She had taken them, along with the riches I had given her, and disappeared."

I gasp, surprised at the betrayal, even though I had been expecting it in the story. The gifts he had given her, I could see, but even the clan treasures? Who had his mate been that she could be so cold?

Verrick's arm comes around me, pulling me down to his chest. "I didn't go after her. I just . . . let her go. If she hated being with me so much, I would not stop her. But more than that . . . I was embarrassed. My mate had shamed me in front of my entire clan. I failed to protect that which was most precious to us and put a viper in our midst. I was rightfully challenged for control of the clan, for the title of Warchief, and I considered letting myself be killed rather than live with such humiliation."

"Oh, Verrick."

He shakes his head. "Obviously, I decided to meet the challengers and I won. I decided that I had been given a gift in the form of experience. That I had been taught a hard, but necessary lesson: women, especially human women, could not be trusted. I resolved to keep my distance for the rest of my life, to make my duty to my clan my only mate."

The weight of what he is saying settles on me and I pull back, looking him in the eyes. "And then you met a human woman that wouldn't stop pursuing you, no matter how much distance you resolved to put between us. Verrick, can you forgive me? I must have reminded you of such a hard time in your life and treated it like a game."

He pulls me back to him, our naked skin pressing against each other. "Truth be told, you captivated me from the first. You are completely unlike Lucy; thoughtful and cheerful, expecting nothing in return. You flirt because you want me, not something that I can give you. The only thing that is the same between you is the fact that you are both human. That was enough to send me running. Honestly . . . you scared me."

Verrick pulls me up and takes my lips in a heated kiss. When we part, I am breathless and can see the lust in his eyes. "I am glad you did not let me run from you, temptress. I've quite enjoyed being caught in your claws."

"My claws, eh?" I respond, scratching my blunt nails down his chest. He groans and I see his hardness swell with readiness under the blanket. "Shall we see how sharp my claws can be?"

Verrick laughs quietly and places a kiss on my forehead.

"Later, temptress," he says against my hair, "You need rest. But tonight, when we are alone, my body is yours for the taking."

I *am* tired. So, obediently, I nod and curl into his side. I've always been a fast sleeper, but here in the wee hours, I slide asleep even more effortlessly than usual.

And my dreams have never been sweeter.

CHAPTER 15

Verrick

I awaken a scant few hours after falling asleep, but I feel energized. Hopeful. Younger, even. Like the weight of years has fallen off of my shoulders, and it is because of the beauty drooling on my shoulder. She did not have the presence of mind to put on her silken wrap and so her hair has gone a bit wild in her sleep, but it doesn't matter. She is still the loveliest thing I have ever beheld, and I have seen the queen, who was blessed by fairies with beauty.

I stretch lightly, but the slight movement jostles Pellia, who grumpily burrows back into my side. "Go back to sleep," she groggily grouches at me, screwing her eyes tight.

"It's morning. Late, I believe."

She groans, then suddenly sits up with a gasp. "No! Late morning? I had another meeting with Antony scheduled." Pellia bolts out of our furs, frenetic with energy, before seeing herself in the mirror and moaning with discouragement.

The human male's name on her lips sours my good mood. "You take an eager interest in pleasing that male."

Pellia merely snorts in reply, massaging some of her sweet-smelling cream into her scalp and fixing her braids. "I take an eager interest in not offending anyone with power to make me regret it."

"If he harmed or bothered you in any way, it would be the last thing he did." I vow, sitting up and stretching out the kinks in my shoulders.

My lover meets my eyes in the mirror, amusement sparkling in her own as she lines them with kohl and applies a golden powder. "That is very sweet of you to say, but all I need to do to manage Antony is meet with him on time and flatter him a little to his face. He's always been easy to deal with."

"So you know him well, then?"

"Very well," she replies, walking nude across the tent to get a new dress from her trunks. The beautiful regent bends over and I am treated to an excellent view. Too excellent. I clear my throat lightly and push down on my unruly cock that has woken up again.

"How do you know him?"

"That is a tale for another time," she says, pulling on a shift and shimmying into another gown. It's a beautiful forest green that reminds me of the trees back home, near my clan lands. I am suddenly hit with a longing to bring Pellia to see them.

Like magic, in just a few moments, Pellia is ready to leave, having transformed from rumpled sleeper to radiant regent in the blink of an eye.

"I'll tell you later," she is saying, all the while headed to the tent flap. Looking over her shoulder, she gives me a smoldering smile, one that does not make it any easier to control my cock. "I'll be visiting his manor house today, but I'll be back by dinner. You can inform me of the day's activities and . . . other things. Later."

Then she is gone, and I am left alone. I consider taking myself in hand to release my pent-up arousal, but already I am spoiled. Anywhere other than Pellia's tight cunt doesn't appeal to me. So I wait a while longer and then move to start my day.

Investigations need to be made.

Though we could not find the spy in our midst yesterday, that does not mean that we are completely without recourse. My orc scouts and I scour the village, finding more orc-made trinkets, including some at the site of the fire we fought when we arrived. How we were supposed to have set and put out the fire, I do not know, but it is merely one more thing to add to the mystery.

But that is not all that we search for. Throughout the town we search for the scent trail of the ifrit oil. It was a mistake by the Cabal to orchestrate a fire when we arrived. If they hadn't done so, then I never would have picked up the method with which they set up their arson. Now that I know the scent, though, I will never stop searching for it until I find the next arsonist.

The sun is high in the sky when one of my scouts, Ossit, comes to me. "Warchief, we've found it, but . . . you should take a look."

Striding after them as fast as I can, they lead me to a barn at the edge of town. The orc scouts are all standing around it, two holding the doors shut for the outside. The telltale stench of ifrit oil curls through the air outside this building, a large quantity of the stuff obviously within.

"What is the meaning of this?" I ask, "Why are they holding the doors closed?"

"One of the undead is within," Ossit answers. "He too was killed by a hex, possibly at the same time as the human yesterday."

"But since we did not know about him, the dark magic has had time to raise him from his grave," I muse grimly. "Is he strong?"

"He appears to have more strength than a regular human, though his flesh is already rotting. It is good that we found him. He appears to be a *stratkthri*, a biter. He would have spread the curse through the town and we would have had an outbreak before long."

I consider my scout's words. "And the ifrit oil?"

"There's a barrel in the back. If we had to guess, I would say that the bottle from yesterday was filled from this barrel."

"So, this human was the source?"

"At least of the ifrit oil."

Which means he probably knew more about the Cabal than Owen. When they found out that we knew about the ifrit oil they decided to clean house, it seems. Frustrating. I do not want to be a step behind this fucking Cabal for one more moment. But it seems that we will not be able to find them out through this avenue and will have to keep following Pellia's plan, dangerous though it may be.

I sigh. "Kill it. Smash in the head and burn it. Then call Hoggins to come and cleanse the barn of dark magic so the hex won't spread and neutralize the ifrit oil so that it can no longer be used. At least we should not have to fight any more fires."

"Yes, Warchief." The surrounding scouts that have heard my words get to work quickly, though not before acknowledging my command with the sign of respect.

I leave them to it, not interested in watching them kill the undead. It is a task most orclings could do. But not most humans. It just continues to show how little regard the Cabal has for their own people that they left such a dangerous creature in their midst. Fucking cowards. I walk back to town, frustrated and maybe even a little angry. Another wasted day searching for shadows and finding none. When I do finally find the Cabal, I swear I will not stop until they are all dead.

❊ ❊ ❊

It's amazing how good sex can fix a disappointing day. I was in a foul mood from my thwarted hunt, barely fit for company. But after dinner, Pellia furtively smiled at me and walked to the tent before me. When I went to meet her, she was already on her knees, ready to suck my soul out through my cock and all thoughts of frustration and disappointment disappeared as we fell into each other.

Many rounds of fucking later, we are laying on my furs, the curvy little human draped on me like another blanket and my fingers trail teasingly up and down her spine, the claws entirely sheathed. I am considering beginning to thrum again for her when I remember she promised me a tale.

"So now will you tell me how you came to know Duke Strand?"

Pellia gustily sighs against me and props her elbows on my chest, holding up her head to look in my eyes. "Must we speak of other men when I am in bed with you?"

"Other men?" I quirk a brow, even as I have to hold back the growl in my chest.

She nods, with a world-weary air that I have never really seen on her before. "Yes. 'Men.' I cannot tell this story without mentioning Yorian as well."

Now the growls come. I couldn't hold them back if I wanted to. "The worm that branded you?"

"Yes. I met him and Antony very close to the same time. Are you sure you want to hear it?"

I nod. "If you want to tell me."

"*Want* is a strong word, but I suppose I do not mind."

She sighs again, and she lays her head on my chest. My arms come around her as she talks.

"I was just a little girl," Pellia begins. "Barely had seen my eighth summer when I first met Yorian. The old king was ailing with no heir and two Houses were vying to be the next king: House Howser and House Strand. My father finagled it so that I would see both the heir candidates during the Council season. He commanded me to play with them, get close to them. He was always strategizing, even then, when I was so young. Now I can see he was trying to make me the next queen. But as a child, I just wanted to play. The two boys that they sent me to befriend were Yorian of House Howser and Antony of House Strand. They were both a little older than me and maybe saw what I didn't: that these were not play dates, but potential future matches. They both became rather possessive of me."

She pauses, burrowing further in my chest. Obligingly, I tighten my arms until she is practically fused with my skin. When she is settled to her satisfaction, she says, "I don't think it was about me, truly. Having the backing of House Santir would strengthen either Houses' bid to the throne and so engaging their respective heirs to me would be advantageous. I'm sure Yorian and Antony were instructed to get close to me as well."

I think Pellia is underestimating her charms. I can imagine the puppy love of two human boys as they met the warm and radiant Pellia. I'm sure they wanted her because of their own attraction towards her, but I don't interrupt her tale.

She continues, "The two of them hated each other, the ancient rivalry of their Houses poisoning their minds against one another. Though, of course, they were genial, even friendly, to each other's faces. As we grew, I felt I was in a tugging match between the two of them. If one had some of my time, the other would then demand the same, but more and better. On and on. Then Yorian was named the heir and our engagement was set. I was seventeen."

Pellia lays her head down over my heart. I feel the firm *thump, thump* of my own chest with her ear pressed against it. More and more it is beating for her. I was right to be wary, but it is too late now. I am already falling into the precipice, the edge long behind me. Pellia doesn't notice the wayward nature of my thoughts, or the heaviness of my cock as it readies itself to take her again. She keeps talking. "Everything was working out according to my father's plan when whispers of a fairy-blessed beauty began flitting through the countryside. They soon made their way to the ears of the court and Yorian himself. Rumor said that Antony, thwarted from taking me, was going to go on a quest to find the beauty and take her for himself. But their young rivalry had never fully rested and Yorian, twenty-two to my nineteen, found her first. Taking one look at the child, he could see the woman that she would grow to be and how she would be the ultimate trophy. He announced that he would marry her when she came of age. But he couldn't let me go either. When I turned twenty, I was informed that I would be Yorian's mistress, and he tucked me away in Garden Manor, thwarting Antony once again."

"Was your father angry that you were not the queen?"

"Oh, he was furious, but he kept it to himself. He still tried to use my position to bring more power to House Santir right up until he was killed in the war. He was one of the first sent to the front with our troops, so I suppose he didn't hide his resentment well enough if Yorian punished him like that."

"And you? Were you disappointed?"

She shakes her head. "I never wanted to be queen. I certainly did not want Yorian. Or Antony, for that matter. I was just trapped. I could not do or say anything without it being reported to Yorian. He was extremely possessive. Once he decided I was his, he would be damned if he let anyone else have me."

Pellia looks up and then to her left and right, as if remembering that she should be more careful with her words. Agents of the Cabal could be listening, even now. Her voice drops to the barest whisper when she admits, "I considered leaving him a time or two, but I always saw something in his eyes that gave me pause and made me reconsider. Some sort of dark madness. It wasn't until later that I found out that he was part of the Cabal that serves Lord Grazrath."

That startles me. I whisper back, "The Cabal seeks to serve the Demon of Pain?"

Pellia holds up her head again, looking into my eyes, still murmuring quietly. "Did no one tell you? The Cabal does all their dark and horrendous deeds in the name of Grazrath. They offer all the pain and suffering they cause as an offering to him. I suppose it makes them feel protected, having the blessing of a terrible demon on their side."

"It did not save them from discovery, nor from the retribution of your queen."

My lover snorts, an endearing sound, and replies in her quiet way, "Well, who's to say if demons are real, anyway? No one has claimed to see one for centuries and those that did were usually quite mad. And if they are real, maybe the fairy magic in Adalind's blood counteracts their dark blessing. Who can tell? But I am glad that they are being hunted down like the vermin they are. None of us can be safe until they are gone."

"Maybe. Or maybe something worse will take their place."

Pellia laughs at me, a merry sound, her voice back to its

regular volume. "Such a dour fatalist! Do you see nothing good in the world?"

I smile at the jibe, the expression feeling a little stilted and unpracticed on my lips, but she brings it out in me. "I'm seeing something good in the world right now," I say, looking directly at her.

She smiles again, bright like the sun, and moves to kiss me again.

And then there is no more talking.

CHAPTER 16

Agony

Traveling the secret path in the Dense Wood, my party and I make excellent time. We should be in Grimblton long before the orc's caravan, giving us plenty of time to reach the secret ritual chamber before our plot.

I look forward to taking the orc and breaking him, hearing his screams as the runes of the forbidden ritual are carved into his flesh. From upstart regent to perfect, writhing sacrifice.

The baying of werewolves in the distances causes my horse to startle slightly beneath me, but I am too experienced a rider to let him throw me. Instead, I take my riding crop to his flank and push him onward. The wretched animal fights me for a moment and the riding crop flashes out from my hand more viciously than before, finally bringing the mount in hand. Nothing will bother us on this path. A powerful witch carved it with dark magic and it is permeated with death. No creature crosses this path if they can help it.

That distraction dealt with, I let my thoughts slide in a more pleasant . . . lascivious direction.

Pellia is still sweet and innocent, no matter her years with Yorian. The more I see her, the more I want her. Want to devour her sweetness and corrupt her innocence. I understand well why Yorian kept her locked away in Garden Manor, away from prying eyes; she is too precious a possession to lose.

But I think Yorian underestimated her as well. She is serving the Cabal with zeal, leading the orc right to his doom. She could have been an ally this whole time, but instead, he kept her in the dark, separate and away from our machinations. *Fool.*

When Pellia is mine, she will be my equal, the shadow queen to my king. We will bathe in the blood of innocents and garner the blessing of Lord Grazrath upon our union. With the power of the ritual behind us, we will turn Adrik into the empire it was meant to be and the world will bow or burn at our feet.

I urge my horse into a gallop, and the party does the same. We must make haste. It would not do to be unprepared for our guests.

CHAPTER 17

Pellia

Our caravan moves out early, just after dawn. With Verrick and mine's nightly activities, I am exhausted, but this time I do not even have to ask whether or not I can ride with Verrick. He merely scoops me up in his arms and mounts his warbeast with the ease of a rider of experience. It is not the most dignified position, but I am beyond caring.

As we are about to start our travel, Bronwyn approaches, looking hesitant. Maybe even embarrassed.

"Regent Santir," she greets, "Regent Verrick, I believe it is time that I bid you farewell."

That makes me sit up in Verrick's saddle. "What do you mean, bid us farewell? Will you not continue the tour with us to Grimblton and the surrounding villages?"

She shakes her head. "I've really been no help so far. You have been better at cataloging the losses than I am and Regent Verrick needs no help with the investigation. After what happened with Owen . . . "

"Surely, you cannot blame yourself for that. You were as betrayed as we were. Moreso, since he was your friend."

Bronwyn frowns. "Even so, I feel responsible. I brought him into your midst, and we still don't know who he was working for or how much information from the investigations and such that he has passed to them. No, I've been thinking about it and talking to Quill and I believe we can do more at home, helping the others prepare for the winter. I thank you for the honor of your invitation to advise you on your tour of the damages, but I believe it must end here.

I go to argue, when Verrick's hand comes to my shoulder, stopping my words. He murmurs in my ear, "Let her go. We know what waits for us in Grimblton and it will probably be better not to have distractions."

His argument makes sense and I sigh. "Very well," I say to Bronwyn. "Though I still do not think that you should blame yourself for Owen's treachery, I understand what you are saying. Thank you for bringing this problem to light and traveling with us all this time. We wish you safe travels back to Aquilar."

Then I remember a past conversation and say, "When we get back to the capital, as thanks for your service, we will make you the official new magistrate of Aquilar, in your father's stead. Look for the letter."

The peasant woman looks shocked, then curtsies deeply, though a little awkwardly, and says, "Thank you for your consideration. I will serve the crown faithfully, Regent Santir."

With that, she leaves and Verrick pulls his mount around, heading southeast along the border of the Dense Wood. I lean back in his arms and begin to doze as we ride, comfortable in the knowledge that Verrick would never let me fall.

The day of travel goes like all the others. We stop in the smaller villages to take stock of their losses and pass out relief supplies. Those supplies are running low. I wish I had magic like Queen Adalind so that I could have cast a vault charm on my bags so that they would never grow empty, since it would connect them to stores in the capital. As it is, the wagons in the caravan are looking rather sad and desolate.

As we travel along the Dense Wood, I keep getting the feeling that something is watching us. I tell myself that I am being foolish, that it's what comes from traveling next to such wild and dangerous place, so I say nothing to Verrick.

Then, just as the sun is setting, we all hear it. The baying of werewolves.

"Circle the wagons!" shouts Verrick, "Protect the humans! Faster! We must outpace them!"

The orcs rush to obey his commands, even as he passes me from his warbeast to Friza's. "Take her to safety. Protect the wagons!"

I realize he's going to ride into the woods toward the danger and reach out a hand. "No! Verrick!"

But he's already gone, riding to battle as Friza takes me further away. The wagons of the caravan have created a circle, the humans huddled in the middle; the guards are running to the outside of the circle, joining the orcs. The Royal Mage is with them, air whipping about him in a fierce hurricane as he readies it to be thrown like invisible blades at our enemies. The baying is closer now, all around us. Friza dumps me rather unceremoniously in the center of the servants and says, "Whatever happens, stay here." Then she is gone as well.

The sound of battle soon rends the air, war cries and screams happening in equal measure. It is hard to see past the wagons, but I try, standing tall amid the cowering servants. I want to see Verrick. He went into battle first, right into the Dense Wood, but the werewolves are here now, fighting the orcs and soldiers protecting us. Does this mean that they avoided him? Or did he fall so soon?

A horrid pit grows in my stomach at the thought of Verrick, wounded or dead. Am I to lose my lover so soon after finally having him?

A splash of blood comes through the protective barriers, staining the ground in droplets. Red, not the orcish black. So human or werewolf. A snarling gets my attention and I whirl around to see an enormous wolf, with a maw like an open cavern, trying to shove its way through the wagons. A second later, an ax is embedded in its skull and it whines before the life goes out of its eyes. Friza appears a moment later, yanking the ax out of the skull and then launching herself back into the fray.

Howling rends the air, each wolf joining in turn. Then I see flashes of fur running back to the wood whence they came and soon an uncanny stillness is in the air. Are they gone? Have we won? I hear shouts for a healer and move out of the way so that he can answer the call, watching him bustle out of the circle with his assistant behind him. Soon after, I hear the human guards whistle, the sound for all clear, and I break into a run, bursting out from behind the safety of the wagons.

Carnage awaits me as I step onto the battlefield. Dead wolves litter the ground, showing that they fared far worse against us than we did them, though I see some of the guards I brought with me lying still as well. I know each of those guards individually, and I try not to think of who might be dead as I move through the bloodbath, looking for one person in particular.

I find Friza, a gash on her arm, and ask, "Friza! Where is Verrick?"

She wordlessly points behind and I turn to see Verrick exiting the woods astride his warbeast, dead wolves on the ground behind him. It looks like he killed three werewolves himself, but I don't care about that now. Black blood pours from a wound on his side and another nasty claw mark mars his left arm.

"Verrick! You're hurt!" I rush to his side.

"I'm fine, little one. They are surface wounds."

"Surface wounds do not bleed so profusely!" I retort hotly. "Healer! Where is the healer?"

Verrick only chuckles, a little weakly, and says, "There's no need for a healer, Pellia. There are those that need him more than I."

"Then come with me," I command. "I can wrap your wound so that the bleeding stops." At least I think I can. How hard can wrapping a bandage be?

"We should move out as quickly as we can," he tells me, not moving to follow my order. "They are gone for now, but they may come back with greater numbers. This first wave could have just been a scouting party."

I didn't think of that. "We are close to the village of Portia. We should ride there and stay for the night. They should have a village wall that can keep out the likes of werewolves."

Verrick nods, looking tired. "We should make haste, then. Though, this means that we will not reach Grimblton tonight as we planned."

"That doesn't matter now," I say. "We need to get everyone to safety. We can worry about our journey later."

Besides, we would just be running right into a trap, I think, *and it would not be good for Verrick to be wounded when we face the Cabal.*

The Warchief turns away from me and shouts, "Alright, round up the dead and wounded into the wagons and move out quickly. We ride for Portia!"

Verrick then puts out his hand and I take it, letting him pull me onto the back of his warbeast. Once atop the mount, I reach out and rip strips from my shift's skirt and press the fabric into my lover's side to staunch the bleeding. He does not so much as wince, though I am pressing most forcefully.

The wagons straighten out as they follow Verrick orders. We will need to burn the dead when we get to safer quarters.

Then we ride, leaving the slaughter behind us.

✳ ✳ ✳

Later we are in a room in the inn at Portia. I fuss over Verrick, much to his apparent amusement. Using a rag, I wash the blood from his body and we wrap his wounds. The slashes on his arm go through one of his tattoos and I exclaim over it.

"Your poor tattoo! When it heals, it won't look quite right."

Verrick snorts. "It's alright. Scars are a warrior's honor. I do not mind them."

"Well, *I* mind them. You could have been killed, Verrick! Why did you ride off into the woods by yourself?"

"I wanted to stop them before they got to the wagons, but there were too many. I'm only sorry that I couldn't kill more of them before they reached the guards. We lost too many today."

His words make me somber. Four guards and one orc died in the attack, quick though it was. I will need to write my personal condolences to their families and see about giving them a hero's pension. If it weren't for them, the wolves might have broken through the wagons and killed so many unarmed people.

Still, I go to wash Verrick's arm before bandaging it and am surprised to find a rough texture under my cloth. More scales?

I take a closer look and notice the tiny texture of scales under each tattoo that I can see.

"Is there a reason that you only have tattoos where there are scales?" I ask.

Verrick touches his forehead, a little self-consciously, I think and responds, "This? A youthful rebellion."

I raise my brows, trying to picture the serious, honorable Verrick as rebellious and fail. I say, "You must have been very young then, for I cannot imagine that now."

With a rueful chuckle, he responds, "Yes, I was not quite an adult, only nineteen. Before I even met Lucy. I ignored the warnings of my father and went to find my mother."

"Oh." The tone of the conversation shifts. I can tell this story does not have a good ending, despite that, I will not stop him if he wants to tell it. I move on with my ministrations, wrapping his arm as I have with his side, mutely listening.

Verrick nods his head. "I was full of all the piss and vinegar of a young orc, ready to slay dragons and make my name. But first, I wanted to see my mother. To meet her and her people."

"And did you? Find her I mean?"

He grimaces, some of the light going out of his eyes. "Yes. It took a month, but I finally found her pod of sirens. They were as beautiful and terrible to behold as my father had always said. When I found the guards that bordered their village they were going to kill me, but one of them noticed I had the markings of a siren-born. They took me to an abandoned island and told me to wait. I was there for hours before my mother finally arrived. I thought she would be happy to see me, glad that I had grown up strong and capable."

"But she wasn't?"

He shakes his head, some old pain on his face. I put my hand on his cheek to comfort him and he nuzzles into it, accepting my offering. "No, she wasn't. I was, apparently, a source of great shame to her. She told me so, and to never come back . . . that next time I encountered any of her pod, she would have them kill me on sight. I was *her* youthful folly, evidence of a time when she was seduced by a non-siren and she wanted to forget me. Especially since she was now mated to the pod chief. I tried to reason with her and she, rather than continuing the argument, screamed at me."

I suck in a breath. Sirens are most known for their songs, the *lures* they use to amuse themselves killing sailors, but it is also known that their screams are deadly. They scramble the brains and burst the blood of all who hear it. They are known as *death screams* for that reason.

He continues, "It was only for a second and I have some resistance to the effects since I am siren-born, but it still felt like nails were shredding the inside of my head. My hands went to my ears to stop the noise and my eyes closed of their own volition. When I opened them again, she was gone."

I tie off his bandage, absorbing what he just told me. "Did she mean to kill you, do you think?"

He shakes his head. "I do not think so. She would have had to scream longer to truly hurt me. I think she just wanted to warn me off. It worked. I went back home, tail between my legs, with a deep anger in my heart. As they rejected me, I wanted to reject them, at least symbolically. And since I could not remove my patches of scales, I had them obscured by tattoos instead."

He shrugs. "Like I said, a youthful rebellion. I do not mind the scales so much now."

Poor young Verrick. My heart bleeds for the hurt he must have carried, the pain of rejection from his own mother. Why would a person have a child only to throw them away? It makes no sense to me, though I suppose I know that the world is complicated. Putting aside my errant thoughts, instead I move to kiss Verrick's lips, trailing my fingers over the unbroken tattoo on his right arm.

He looks surprised. "What was that for?"

I smile and give another quick, teasing kiss. "Has no one ever comforted you after telling a hard tale before?"

Verrick shakes his head slowly. Oh, well, now I want to comfort him more. I take his face in my hands and slowly, gently, give him another kiss. There's nothing lustful or passionate about it. It's a caress, the solace of one soul giving support to another. Somehow, though, as it progresses, it still leaves me breathless as I part from him.

For a moment, Verrick regards me with deep, inscrutable eyes, and then we are kissing again. This time with tongue and little nips of teeth and tusk. I feel myself respond to his ardor, growing wet between my thighs. The orc Warchief groans, hauling me closer until I'm sitting on his lap.

"Always so hungry for your orc," he growls against my lips, then captures them again in a searing kiss. I swear, if I weren't sitting, my legs would buckle.

"That's not why I did this!" I protest, even as I kiss him back, tracing my tongue against his in a flirtatious sign that he takes, plundering my mouth with his tongue.

"Is it not?" he asks, hands coming behind my dress to pull at the laces of my dress and the brooches at my shoulders.

That gives me pause. "Verrick! You are hurt! You can't possibly think . . ."

"I can," he says, smoldering at me, "I can when I smell your arousal this strongly, even through your *orikiri* leaf tea. You *need* me."

Then his lips find my neck and almost all the thoughts fly out of my head. He pulls the dress and shift down my body and soon I am sitting on him naked while he is still fully clothed. I move to pull at his buckle, but he stills my hand.

"Patience, temptress. I have other games I want to play."

Verrick, the most serious male I know, wants to play games. I look at him in surprise and a slow smile grows over his features. I feel myself becoming wetter just looking at him. He takes me and throws me down on the bed. I squeal in surprise as I bounce against the mattress and then laugh at his playfulness. Who is this orc?

Verrick leans over me, his chest barely rubbing against my nipples, and says, "Alright temptress, you have teased and tormented me for so long. It's my turn now. You are not allowed to come until I give you leave, alright?"

I open my mouth to protest when he begins to thrum, harder and louder than I have ever heard it before. Without even touching me, I feel myself growing wetter and wetter, the pleasure rising in my clit and deep in my core. Higher and higher, and then suddenly he stops right before my peak. I groan in frustration and buck my hips toward his, trying to find friction to ease my ache, but he just moves away slightly and chuckles darkly.

"No, temptress, not yet."

Then he is thrumming again, and again I feel myself rising to the peak, only to be thwarted at the last minute. On and on this goes, with his thrumming teasing out my pleasure, only to be denied my orgasm. My body is on fire, every nerve sensitized. I buck and writhe and wail, but still he torments me.

Finally, I can take it no longer and my hands dive to my core, wanting to give myself the release that my body is screaming for. But Verrick's powerful hands grab mine and hold them over my head in an iron grip.

"Naughty temptress. That cunt is *mine*, and I didn't give you leave to touch it, did I?"

I whimper. "Please Verrick, no more! I can't take it anymore!"

"Yes temptress, you can. And you will."

The torture starts again, this time made more intense with Verrick holding me down. I cry out, begging and pleading as he thrums. Over and over. The minutes bleed together and soon

I could not tell you how long he has kept edging me toward release and then denying me. All I am capable of is *feeling*, every part of my body becoming an erogenous zone.

Finally, Verrick growls, a pleased and aroused sound. "Remember this feeling, temptress. Remember who mastered your body for your pleasure. And remember that this cunt is mine, to do with as I please."

Then his fingers are pushing into me, and with just that one touch, I am coming. Coming harder than I ever have before, my back bowing off the bed. He pumps his fingers into my pussy, once, twice, three times, and then I feel his cock replacing them, sliding through my gushing release into my tight sheath. And I'm coming again and again, as if every orgasm he denied me are all coming at once, the moments bleeding together. Time loses all meaning again, until I am a replete quivering body underneath him as he comes as well, roaring his release.

He collapses next to me and pulls me toward him, my back to his front. His fingers trace lightly over my skin, claws sheathed, and I shiver, even those little touches feeling like too much after the teasing he put me through.

When I am finally capable of speech again, I say, voice hoarse, "I had no idea that orcs could do that with just their *sibilance*."

Behind me, he quietly laughs, his hand resting possessively on my thigh. "Few can. My *sibilance* is stronger than any orc I've ever met, a gift of my mother's heritage. The siren's *lure* and the orc's *sibilance* marry well together."

"Does that mean that you can scream like a siren as well?" I shiver at the thought.

He shakes his head. "I've never done a death scream. Perhaps that is just because I've never had to; my skill with my blade is deadly enough. But I don't think that is one of the gifts I inherited. Just my version of *lure*."

"At least she did not leave you with nothing, then."

I feel, rather than see, Verrick grow serious again and regret my words instantly. Why did I say that? My only excuse is that I still feel addled and lust-drunk.

But then he replies, "Yes, though she didn't want me, I still have her gifts. I suppose I should thank her for that."

"You do not need to thank her for anything," I retort, turning around so that our fronts are pressed together and I stare into my lover's eyes. "You are the one that made something of yourself and mastered your gifts. Where they come from is of little consequence."

He stares back at me, his eyes again inscrutable, then gives me a sweet, chaste kiss.

"Sleep now, little one," he says. "It's been a long day, and you were right: with these wounds I'm going to need rest."

Already my eyelids are growing heavy, even as he says the words. Our game tonight took a toll on my body.

So, in my lover's arms, and well-fucked, I fall asleep.

CHAPTER 18

Verrick

The morning comes swiftly after bouts of unfulfilling sleep. The soreness in my side plagues me and I suspect Pellia was right when she said that I shouldn't have fucked her in my condition. But I have no regrets, even as the wound distracts me all night. It probably opened during the end of our game when I pounded into her sweet cunt with abandon.

I do not mind the sleeplessness. Instead, I hold Pellia in my arms as she twitches and murmurs in her sleep, dreaming deeply. At one point she sleepily mumbles, "Eggs for that price? It's robbery . . ." before turning and snuggling deeper into my side. I could watch her for hours and never be bored. But soon I feel it is close to dawn and time to rise and prepare for our departure.

Carefully, so as not to wake the sleeping beauty, I extricate myself from the bed. I stretch, feeling the pain of my wounds as I move through my normal routine. I don't even wince, however, even as they make their complaints known. My tolerance for pain is high, and I have been trained by my father to never show pain. Showing pain puts you in a position of vulnerability and can mean your death on the battlefield.

Instead, I wordlessly change my bandages, amused at how much cloth Pellia used to cover me. She is obviously not trained in healing, although I enjoyed her ministrations and fussing over me. With clean bandages and a liberal amount of healing tincture to stave off infection spread over the wounds, I exit the room and head downstairs.

It's still dark as I enter the common room, though the light of a fire glows in the kitchen, the innkeeper's wife already up to cook breakfast for their unexpected guests. Silently, I exit and find Friza and my orcs already outside, quietly preparing the caravan to leave.

I address Friza, keeping my voice low. "How goes the watch? Anything to report?"

The orcress shakes her head. "It was quiet. The wolves didn't follow us. I think they attacked the caravan because they were desperate. The bodies of those we killed looked skinny, weak. Mayhap there is something affecting their hunting in the Dense Wood. They were probably after our supplies."

Snorting, I say, "If only werewolves weren't so stubborn about keeping their independence. If they were a part of Adrik, they could apply for the supplies and I'm sure with Pellia's bleeding heart, she would send them stores quickly. In fact, if they had come to us in their humanoid form and asked, Pellia probably would have given them what we have left."

Friza looks amused. "Expounding on the virtues of your mate? So soon after running away from her because you couldn't trust that she was as she appeared."

"She's not my mate," I growl.

My second shrugs. "Semantics. She will be, I'm sure, when you are through stubbornly resisting the Instinct."

Is that what I'm doing? I thought I had given in to it, but I think about it for a moment. Pellia as my mate, my bite on her shoulder, forever in my life and my bed. Instead of the panic I expect, a sense of peace settles over me. My Mating Instinct purrs, pleased at the hypothetical scenario.

But now is not the time to be thinking of such things. I banish my daydreams and say, changing the subject, "Gather all the supplies and wake the humans. We should leave soon if we want to get to Grimblton by noon."

Friza laughs. "Oh yes, wouldn't want to be late to *Grimblton*." She says the town name meaningfully and I send her a sharp look. We still don't know who is listening, *how* they are listening, and we are supposed to be in the dark about the trap. She merely shrugs again and wanders off to obey my orders.

I glance back at the inn, up to the rooms where the windows are dark, my thoughts once again straying to Pellia. To her sleeping form, naked in the blankets. Her hair will be wild again after another night of forgetting her silk wrap, and she'll have to spend extra time fixing it with her oils and creams. I can imagine her dismay when she awakens and sees herself in the mirror, and I allow my lips to curl slightly at the thought.

Well, if it is time for the humans to awake, then maybe I'll go wake my human. Perhaps there will even be time to taste my lover before we have to leave. Maybe even to wake her with my head between her thighs. My Mating Instinct likes that thought.

So slowly I make my way back to where Pellia sleeps, a mission in mind.

❋ ❋ ❋

There is no time for tasting. My plan is thwarted when Pellia wakes on her own, and, just as I predicted, is horrified at her appearance. She moves frantically around the room, preparing for the day and fixing her hair. At one point, she pulls out a potion that smells of magic and alchemy and smoothes it into her braids, which are instantly tamed into silky plaits. Then she dresses for the day, concealing her luscious body under layers of fabric.

Later, I determine. Later, when we are alone, I will hold her down and lick her cunt until she comes at least three times on my tongue. That thought makes me smile inwardly, but I keep a stone face as we move out, a wary watchfulness as we move toward Grimblton. Not only could more danger be coming from the woods, but also there is danger ahead of us.

The Cabal. They wait for us in their web, ready to strike. Though we have a plan to counter them, I would be wise to be

...e ready, in case they strike when they are not expected, or if they suspect Pellia is not with them and leave her out of their plans. Or target her instead. The thought makes my blood run cold, turning to icy fear in my veins.

Is Friza right? Is Pellia my mate? My protectiveness would seem to indicate yes, but I am unsure. I thought Lucy was my mate before and chose poorly. Maybe Pellia is just meant to be my lover, a temporary dalliance that sates both our lusts and then we pass like ships in the night.

My Mating Instinct doesn't like the way my thoughts are heading. It growls in my head and gnashes its teeth thinking of Pellia. *Mine*, it says forcefully. *Mine!*

I am distracted for the last half of our journey, so it is good that it is uneventful. We arrive at Grimblton, greeted by the now familiar smell of burnt wheat in the air. There are less scorched fields here than there were in Aquilar and Kingsbury, but they are still there, a testament to the depravity of the Cabal.

Pellia turns around in front of me of my warbeast and says, "We can stay at Castle Grimble while we are here. It has been empty since the fall of House Grimble and has the space we need."

I nod, but am wary. I lean down and whisper, "We suppose it is empty, but it is also the most likely place for the Cabal to be holed up."

"A fair point. Should we look elsewhere for lodging? Set up our tents again?"

I consider it but then shake my head, "If we go where we are not expected, then it may throw their plans off kilter. Better to head into the belly of the beast and face them than hide somewhere else, like a coward."

Pellia laughs. "Spoken like a true orc Warchief."

We come to Castle Grimble and find the gardens a little overrun, after a month of no one tending to them, but other than that the austere structure looms over us, the windows dark. It looks quite abandoned.

But looks can be deceiving.

"We set up camp here!" I order. "Tents in the gardens for the soldiers. The regent and I, as well as the servants, will stay in the castle."

"You heard the Warchief," bellows Friza. "Move!"

Pellia slides down off of my warbeast, a little clumsily as it's not like a horse, and says, "I'll head into the keep with the servants. We'll see to dinner and the lodging arrangements."

I nod and reply, "Go. I'll find you later."

She nods and heads into the castle, dark doorways yawning open in front of her like an open mouth. As she disappears into the dark, swallowed by the shadows, I get a foreboding feeling. Like something terrible is going to happen. I couldn't live with myself if that thing that happened was to Pellia.

I dismount my warbeast and move into the ordered chaos of the camp being set up. I'm looking for one orc in particular. When I find him I call out, "Korovi!"

The other orc jogs over to me, "Warchief?"

Korovi is one of the best fighters and scouts in my entire clan. Loyal, too, almost to a fault. If he weren't, I think he could challenge me for Warchief and I'm not sure who would survive. He is also one of the few orcs that I confided in about the true purpose of this mission. He is perfect for my purposes.

"A word," I say, jerking my head to the right, indicating a place away from the rest.

Korovi follows me, and when we are alone, I say in Orikesh. "I need you to protect the regent. We are in the lair of our enemy, and I don't trust that she'll be able to stay safe."

The other orc nods slowly and says, "It would honor me to be the guard of your mate."

That is the second time today she has been referred to as my mate. "She is not my . . . nevermind. I will need more than your word. I would have your Oath."

An orc's Oath is a serious thing. When made to their Warchief, only death or their clan leader can release them from it or they will go to the Nether without honor. Korovi looks surprised, but when he sees how serious I am, he nods, matching my mood with his own seriousness.

"My Oath, Warchief. I will see to the regent's protection, or I will die trying. She will be safe with me."

"I accept your Oath. Know that I do not ask this lightly, Korovi. I trust you above all others with this. Do not fail me."

He places both of his fists on his chest, grim determination on his features, "I will not fail you, Warchief. Leave it to me."

✳ ✳ ✳

Later Pellia and I are set up in a guest chamber, the servants we brought with us having replaced the dusty bedding and set a cheerful blaze in the fireplace. We are finally alone again and my plan from earlier in the morning can take form.

Turning to Pellia, I put a growl in my voice and say, "Get on the bed, temptress."

My lover looks surprised at my sudden action, but a delighted gleam is in her eye as she slowly backs up to the bed, obeying my command.

"Tell me," I say, stalking forward and then leaning over her form, "when I lift your skirts, will I find you wet?"

I skim her jawline with my nose, inhaling the intoxicating scent of her burgeoning arousal.

"Lift them," she says coquettishly, "and find out."

I grin. "Naughty, naughty temptress."

I do as I am bid, slowly sinking to my knees as she perches on the end of the bed. I take her silky skirts in my hands before diving beneath them. Pellia laughs in surprise, but that laugh soon gives way to a choked moan as I find her center. *Ambrosia.* Her wet pussy tastes of earth and honey, a willing, lusty woman. Boldly, I lick her seam again, before finding her clit and sucking lightly. Her hips buck against my face and, encouraged, I do it again. Her needy whimpers spur me on as I lave and suck and thrust my tongue, each action met with a new gush of wetness.

I sheathe my claws and push two fingers into her warm, slippery cunt. Feeling around, I find the rough bit of flesh just behind her entrance and curl my fingers at the same time as I suck her clit again. Her orgasm takes her by surprise, I can tell, as she falls back onto the bed, her hips and back bowing as she cries out my name. But I am not done with her yet. I add another finger and begin to pump mercilessly inside her, drawing out her climax. Just when it seems like she is coming down again, I curl my fingers again and lick her hard, and she is coming again.

Two more times I make her come before she finally pulls her skirts off of my head, pulling me up to kiss me passionately, tasting herself on my lips and tongue.

"Fuck me, Verrick," she commands boldly. "I want to feel you inside me when next I come."

With pleasure, I think, before kissing her again, sweeping my tongue into her mouth and drinking my fill of her passion. I take her, pushing her back into the mattress, and drop my warkilt.

Then the thought occurs to me that we still need to be wary of the Cabal. They could be watching or listening at this very moment. The thought cools some of my ardor. I will share no part of Pellia with anyone, especially not those honorless sadists.

From the corner of my eye, I spy a blanket at the foot of the bed and grab it, placing it over both of us. Pellia raises her brows in a question, but I do not answer. Instead, I bear her down and toss up her skirts, exposing her center to me. Only to me.

I bring my turgid length to her womanhood and slowly, leisurely, I enter. My lover groans at the invasion, her head tossed back in ecstasy, my name once again on her lips. But I make us both wait, drawing out the pleasure of my intrusion until I'm finally seated to the root in her and my eyes roll back slightly at the hot rapture of her squeezing cunt.

Then she says, "Take me, Verrick. Fill me up like the warrior you are," and my control snaps.

With a mighty thrust, I pull out and push back into her, getting faster and faster. Soon she is coming again, this time on my cock, but I am a beast possessed and I grant her no quarter.

Soon I am moving in and out like a crazed, wild thing and she is coming again and again and still I am going. In the haze of my lust, I see her neck and I am overcome with the temptation to bite down, to Claim Pellia, to make myself hers forever. But it is not time, and she has not said yes to forever, so instead I lick and suck the area, bruising with my kisses.

I rip open the bodice of her dress, freeing her breasts and taking each nipple in turn, sucking hard. All the while I am pounding into her, the pressure for release building in blinding pleasure. I am everywhere, kissing and licking and sucking, leaving my mark all over her brown, beautiful skin.

Pellia screams, another climax taking her and finally, finally, I let go, my own climax taking me so hard that I swear my life-force is being sucked out through my cock. Her welcoming channel milks me dry and I collapse to my forearms, barely with enough strength to keep my bulk from crushing her curvy frame.

I roll to my side and she comes with me, laying in my arms, breathing hard, a small smile lighting her gorgeous face, her body calm and replete with sated lust.

We are laying in comfortable silence, when the thought takes me that I am a fool. Of course, Pellia is my mate. I can no longer live without this woman. I don't want to. I know it is fast, but I think I've been feeling this way for a long time and just hid it from myself. My Mating Instinct purrs with approval.

"Pellia," I say, speaking the truth in my heart, "I am falling in love with you."

She does not react the way I expect. She stiffens in my arms and goes pale. "What?"

"I am falling in love with you, Pellia. I think I have been for a while now."

She laughs nervously and says, "You must be mistaken. This is just passion, just sex. Since you have not had a lover in so long, you must be mixing them together. It's understandable."

I get a little annoyed at her continued denial, but I keep my tone even when I reply, "No. I know the difference between lust and love. I feel both for you. I want to be with you, always."

"But . . . but you said that you didn't want a mate! You said
—!"

"I know what I said, but I was lying to myself. I think I've known for quite some time that you are my mate, my true mate. I want to Claim you—"

"No! No Claiming!" she says, suddenly panicked and wrenching away. "I belong to myself. Only me!"

"That's not—"

"No, stop!" she commands, looking at me with tears in her eyes. "Why did you have to ruin this? I wanted a lover, not another owner!"

Now I am starting to get angry, "That is not what Claiming means!"

"Yes, it is!" she yells, pulling her clothes back on as she drifts further and further away from me. "I have been 'claimed' before, if you have forgotten." She gestures between her breasts, now hidden again with fabric. At the brand we both know sits there.

She shakes her head, anger and fear both in her voice as she cries, "Never again. *Never* again!"

The door slams behind her, leaving me in silence in the room. The Mating Instinct pushes me to follow her, to explain, to bring her back. But my pride stills my movement. If she doesn't want me, she will not have me.

Like she said. Never again.

CHAPTER 19

Pellia

I find another room to stay in, though it is cold and musty since it has been empty for so long. Still, I cannot bring myself to wake the servants to fix it for me. I try the bed, but I can't relax. All night I am restless, unable to sleep. Verrick's words ring in my ears, his expressions burned into my eyes, never leaving me at peace, even for a moment. Why did he say that? Why couldn't he keep things the way they were? They were fine, great, perfect, even, before he had to destroy them with his talk of love and Claiming.

The morning comes and I am quick to leave the castle. Anything to get some distance from Verrick and his proclamations of love. I hurry into town, only to find I am being followed.

I whirl around to find Korovi behind me, keeping a respectful distance, his face as unreadable as stone.

"Why are you following me?" I demand, no patience left in me for pleasantries.

The orc's face stays impassive, a soldier's face, when he says, "I've been assigned to your protection."

"Been assigned? When?"

"My Warchief told me yesterday that I am not to let you out of my sight and I will obey."

Verrick ordered him to my protection? Obviously, before our fight. I huff, annoyed. "Nothing will happen to me. You don't need to watch me."

Korovi doesn't respond. He simply stands, a little on the balls of his feet, as if ready to walk the moment I move.

I try a different approach. "I would rather be alone. Please."

The orc shakes his head, then says, "That is unfortunate because I have my orders and I will follow them. Please don't make this more difficult than it needs to be."

I want to yell in frustration. I was looking to be alone today in town, away from orcs and mating and Claims and anything that reminded me of them. I was going to pass out the rest of our supplies and blissfully avoid my personal problems. But it seems that I am over-ruled by a high-handed orc ex-lover who is being far too careful.

But I don't scream or shout or throw any sort of tantrum, tempting though it might be. I just turn on my heel and keep walking into town, my orc shadow trailing behind me.

The day is busy. Though Grimblton has not been hit quite as harshly by the arsonists, they were one of the first towns that had to flee when the orcs invaded during the war, close as they are to Fort Attis. As such, their crops were untended longer than others in the south and their harvest looks grim as a matter of course. The supplies go quickly and we are cleaned out by noon. With nothing else to distract me, I go to sit behind the magistrate's house with an apple and some bread, wanting a few moments of peace without interacting with anyone. This is, of course, ruined by Korovi standing like a statue, watching me from mere paces away.

I fight the urge to scowl. I hold up my meager repast and say, "I am only eating lunch. You can go rest yourself. No need to watch me every minute."

"Orcs can go much longer than humans without eating or resting," is all that he replies.

My annoyance grows, and finally, I have had enough. "Well, Korovi, since you insist on being here when I wanted to be alone with my thoughts, you may stand there and listen to my thoughts instead."

Korovi remains impassive, though I think I detect a hint of unease in his eyes. But I am far beyond caring.

So I begin, "Why is it that males always must lay ownership of something? Why can they not enjoy things for what they are?"

The orc guard looks confused, but I am building up steam and I continue, "Me, for example. Why can I not exist without some male claiming me? Putting the stamp of ownership on me and wanting to take away all my freedom and independence? And wrapping it all up in the trappings of *love*." I sneer at the last word, unable to keep my feelings out of my voice.

"That's not what Claiming is. Or love," responds Korovi, voice stern. His words are an eerie echo of Verrick's last night and they make me explode.

"Yes, it is! Do you think I don't know what *claiming* is? I have had one male already *claim* me. He put his mark on my body and soul, shoved me into a backwater manor so that he could see me whenever he wished, do whatever he wished. Like I was a doll! Some object for him to put away or take out of a cabinet whenever he desired! Nothing was my own. I existed for his pleasure and nothing else! I was owned as surely as a slave, with as many rights over my body as one. And always as he took me and used me, he would speak of love! That is what claiming is! It is a prison without bars and without hope! I was only free when he died!"

My voice rings out through the empty yard, my voice having grown louder than I was expecting. But all my feelings rushed out like poison from a wound and I do not think I could have stopped it if I tried.

There is a small, awkward silence between Korovi and me, my words hanging in the air when Korovi says, carefully, "That may be what claiming is among humans. But that is not how it is with orcs."

Deflated after my rant, I have no energy to argue with him. "What do you mean?" I ask, exasperated that he seems like he wasn't listening.

But Korovi says, "Claiming among my people is an act of trust. It binds us to another person, not the other way around."

"That makes no sense."

The orc nods and continues, "That may be so. But it is true. When orcs Claim another, it makes it so that we can only have children with that chosen partner. If that partner leaves, we suffer the wasting sickness, but the non-orc is just fine. It makes us vulnerable in ways that we are not without the Claim. Even so, in our souls, we feel the call to do so. You could say that rather than us Claiming our mates, we are asking them to Claim us, to make us theirs. That is what the Claiming bite is."

His words rock through me. I had heard of orc Claiming mates before, but never had the effects been laid out so plainly before me. Is he right? Is that what Verrick was asking? To be made mine, to give himself to me in an act of trust?

But Korovi is not done. "And love . . . it *is* a prison. But not one that you would ever willingly leave. It is a wealth of feeling that makes it so that you place another's happiness above your own, where you would sacrifice all that you are and would ever be so that the one you love can be safe and happy. Whatever feeling that other male had for you . . . it was not love or he would have let you go rather than see you suffer. His words were lies, maybe even to himself."

I feel like I can't breathe. It's like Korovi has looked into my soul and ripped open wounds I didn't even know that I had. If Yorian's love was a lie . . . if it wasn't love, no matter what he said . . . does that mean that Verrick . . . does he love me the way Korovi described? Is that what he meant?

I think of Verrick feeling like that about me and I begin feeling a longing and . . . guilt. I rejected him in no uncertain terms. I told him that he was like Yorian, that his wanting to Claim me ruined everything between us. But if he meant it the way Korovi is saying that he did . . . it changes everything.

I open my mouth to respond, though I do not know what I am going to say, when suddenly Friza enters the backyard where we are, flanked on either side by two orcs I don't recognize.

Her eyes are ablaze and everything about her posture says that something is wrong.

She looks at me and points.

"Take her," Friza orders and the two orcs hurry toward me, only to be stopped by Korovi. I shrink back, alarmed. What is happening?

"Stand down Korovi," orders Friza, colder and with more steel than I have ever seen her.

"I've been ordered by the Warchief to protect the regent. I will do that even against you." Korovi growls.

"Those orders are forfeit. Move aside, or I will move you." Friza glares at Korovi.

I break in, trying to diffuse the situation, all the years of diplomacy that have been hammered into me coming to play. "Can we not sort this out peacefully? What is going on? I can help without being detained." Internally, I am fuming. I reject Verrick's Mating Claim and he sends Friza to do this to me? Was I wrong about him? So soon after Korovi convinced me I might have been in the wrong?

Friza ignores me, pulling out an ax, and Korovi does the same.

"My orders can only be countermanded by the Warchief himself. He made me swear an Oath, Friza."

The orcress winces. "Be that as it may, I am taking the regent. Now."

She launches herself toward my protector and steel rings out against steel. This is madness! What is making Friza act this way?

Korovi feints and attacks with the butt of his weapon, obviously going for a non-lethal blow, but Friza parries and attacks with the blade, not holding his same compunctions. Then the other two orcs join in and it is Korovi against three. He is skilled, one of the most skilled fighters I've ever witnessed, but even he will not survive such an onslaught.

"Stop!" I cry. "Stop it! I will go with you willingly. Korovi, stand down and let them take me!"

This halts the battle for a moment, long enough for my protector to be distracted and Friza launches forward, bringing the butt of her ax down on the back of Korovi's neck, who crumples. I cry out, going toward him, but am stopped by the two orcs who are now on either side of me, grabbing my arms in iron grips.

"He needs a healer!" I exclaim, looking at Friza.

She regards me with cold eyes, eyes that almost seem to have hatred in them. "He'll be fine." Still, she glances at one of her companions and jerks her head. "Take him to the healer's and then detain him when he wakes. I can't have him interrupting." Friza turns back to me. "There. He's not the one you should worry about, anyway."

"What is the meaning of this?" I seethe. "I want to see Warchief Verrick now! This is utter nonsense."

Friza steps forward, sinister intent in her body language. "That's just the thing, *Regent*," she spits the word like it is poison. "Warchief Verrick is missing and you are going to tell me where he is, or you will die."

CHAPTER 20

Verrick

The world swims into view as blackness retreats from my eyes. Where am I? What happened? Dull pain throbs through my head and shoulders.

It is quickly apparent that I am in a cell and am chained to a wall with heavy iron chains. I test my muscles against their weight and find my limbs sluggish, though whether that is from whatever is making me so groggy or from how tight my bonds are, I cannot say.

I try to remember what I was doing before I awoke here, but my memory is a yawning chasm, a void where there are no answers. It is easy to deduce that I have been drugged and I remember that the plan the Cabal had for me was to drug me before taking me, that Pellia was meant to administer the draught. But wasn't she going to switch it out with something harmless? Does this mean that Pellia has betrayed me? That she is like Lucy, rotten at the core and I couldn't see it?

But no, something tells me that isn't right. Pellia . . . she wasn't there last night. My memory is filled with gaps, the potion they used obviously strong, but I recall that Pellia and I fought last night. That she left the room and never came back. I went to sleep and . . . woke here.

They must have drugged me somehow while I slept. Something spurred them to move early. Maybe the fact that we were staying in Castle Grimble, on their turf, made them feel threatened. I am only glad then that Pellia was not with me when they came. The Cabal might have her right now as well. They believe she is on their side, but how long could she keep up that facade before they figured out the truth? She would be in danger, and I could never countenance that.

My vision finally clearing enough that I can see, I look out at the room where I am captured and see through the bars into a torture chamber. Implements of pain of all kinds are placed where they are easily seen and, by the smell of blood and death in the air, are well-used. Other cells line walls, almost like a depraved gallery set up to watch the acts of sadism performed in the center of a room. Probably meant as mental torture for the waiting prisoners, seeing what fate is in store for them. The cells are blessedly empty. If I have been taken, I have at least been taken alone. None of my orcs are in this predicament with me.

If they mean to frighten me with the view, however, my captors are gravely mistaken. I lived through the reign of two tyrants before my current king killed his father and took his throne. It would not be the first time that I have witnessed torture and it would not be the first time that I have experienced pain. I will not break.

The door opens and two robed and masked figures enter the room, one tall and the other shorter. Their masks are different, one in the shape of a raven and the other, on the shorter figure, a human skull. Both are dipped in gold, gaudy and ornate. The raven masked figure sees me and smiles.

"Ah, our guest of honor is awake. Looks like the sleeping potion doesn't work as long on orcs."

The skull masked figure nods, "His constitution is strong. He will make a fine offering."

An offering? What are they talking about? I grunt and say, my tongue still slightly slurred from their drugs, "If you meant to kill me as a threat to my king, it will not work."

The robed figures merely laugh. The raven says, "A threat to your king? Is that what you think is happening here? Oh, orc, you have no idea what is in store for you or your king. But you are right about one thing: things for you will only end with your death."

I growl lightly, an instinctual response that I can't help, but this only spurs the two to laugh again.

"Listen to the beast growl as he is caged. It is a pity we can't play with him before the ritual. He would be most diverting."

"Yes," agrees the skull mask, "but we must save all his pain for Lord Grazrath. You'll make quick work of him when the time comes."

"Yes, but it would be so lovely to draw it out. Perhaps we will do so. Lord Grazrath enjoys a display of suffering, does he not?" The raven smiles, as if the thought amuses him.

"So the profane scriptures say," responds the skull.

"Then we will perform the ritual and after, when we are meant to sacrifice an enemy to Lord Grazrath's power, we will make a show of it before the entire Cabal. In fact, we should invite Pellia as well. She would probably like to see her vengeance firsthand."

That brings me up short. "Pellia?"

The raven laughs again. "Oh, you stupid creature. You did not seriously think that a beauty like Pellia was truly interested in you? Sad monster, she was only sleeping with you to distract and lure you here on our orders. And she did so while hating you and your kind to her very core."

So the Cabal still trusts Pellia. Good. They won't try to harm her. I play along and growl again, an angry sound. "You lie!"

"No human could possibly want to fuck a grotesque creature like an orc without an ulterior motive. Even the traitor queen who gave our country to the barbarian horde only did so to save her own neck and crown. You dull monsters are so easy to manipulate, desperate as you are for the love of something more beautiful than yourselves. Love that is impossible to give to a barbarous creature like yourself!"

His words actually land, fresh as I am from my argument with Pellia, where she rejected my declarations of love. So I

let my dismay show on my face, since that is what he w
and both figures only laugh again, thinking that their plan nas
worked exactly as they intended.

The raven turns to the skull and says, "Bring Pellia. The
ritual will need to start as soon as the sun sets, and we wouldn't
want her to miss our triumph."

The skull bows and exits the room, leaving me alone with
the raven, who turns back to me. I pull at the chains, but find
that my strength still seems sapped. The raven says, "Don't
even bother trying to escape. Those are Hex Chains. They steal
your strength and imbue it in the steel. The stronger you are,
the stronger the chains become. There is no escaping what is
coming for you."

He turns to leave, calling over his shoulder, "So be a
good monster and wait, will you? We want you fresh for Lord
Grazrath." The raven leaves through, shutting the door behind
him, and I am alone again, with my thoughts. Lovely.

Uselessly, I pull at the chains again, testing what he says
and with each pull I do seem to get weaker, so I stop. The Cabal
and their dark magics have me. There is no escape.

And soon they will have Pellia. I only hope she is as good at
lying as I once thought she was.

It'll be the only way she will survive what's coming.

CHAPTER 21

Pellia

"What do you mean, Verrick is missing?" I ask, a feeling of dread creeping up in my veins.

"Just that," Friza replies. "His scent is in the room you both slept in last night and then it's gone. No trail."

"I didn't sleep in that room last night. We . . . I . . . slept elsewhere." Something about this doesn't seem right. "We should check the camp. Maybe he is concealing his scent for some reason?" I ask, that same dread growing in me.

"Already done. He's nowhere to be found in the camp or village. No one has seen him since before last night." Friza looks at me, a shrewd expression on her face. "The last thing I knew was a plan that involved you and a fake kidnapping, but now he's gone in truth and your involvement is extremely suspicious."

"My involvement?" I parrot back dumbly. "Surely you can't be serious. I have no reason to mean him any harm."

"So we'll see," Friza says, then barks the order. "Bring her! She needs to be questioned!"

I am dragged away by the remaining orc, his bruising strength digging into my arm, but I barely notice the pain. Where could Verrick have gone? That he is missing is nothing short of alarming. Friza's right that the kidnapping was supposed to be fake, but what if the Cabal moved early? What if they have him now?

No, I mustn't think such thoughts. He's fine. There must be an explanation. He'll turn up soon and resolve this misunderstanding.

I am brought back to Castle Grimble and taken down, down the stone steps into a part of the castle I have never seen before: the dungeon. Once there, I am patted down by Friza, two hairpins and my hidden dagger confiscated, before I am thrown rather unceremoniously into a cell, landing on the floor amongst the rotting straw. The prison door slams shut behind me. My knee aches from the force of the fall, but even that pain cannot distract me from my worry over Verrick's safety. I stand up and whirl around, seeing Friza on the other side of the barred door, and exclaim, "This is a waste of time! While you are interrogating me, you could be looking for Verrick! He could be in danger."

"Which is why I am not wasting time playing games and running around directionlessly. I'm coming right to the source."

"What am I the source of?" I demand, stepping up so that I am right behind the bars, as close to Friza as I can get. "Why do you think I know anything? I'm as much in the dark as you are!"

Friza also steps close to the bar, a threatening look on her face. "You know what happened last night. The scents left in your room . . . there was arousal and then anger and despair. Then nothing else. What could distress My Warchief, if not betrayal?"

Despair? Verrick was so distraught last night that the scent lingered for Friza to find. A pang of guilt darts through my heart, and Friza suddenly inhales deeply, her eyes widening. Then she bangs on the bars of the door, startling me.

"You made a mistake not drinking your *orikiri* leaf tea this morning. I can smell all your emotions clearly. What are you so guilty of? What are you hiding?"

Ah, godsdamn it. I was in such a hurry to leave this morning and avoid Verrick that I forgot to drink my tea, and now Friza is misinterpreting everything. "It's none of your business!" I exclaim. "It's personal and has nothing to do with Verrick being missing. I'm innocent. Surely, if you can smell my feelings of guilt, you can smell that I am not lying."

"Perhaps. But you could be a very skilled liar. Verrick kept saying that you reminded him of Lucy and I thought he was being ridiculous, but now . . ."

"Oh, for all the gods' sakes, I am nothing like Lucy. I mean Verrick and your clan no harm. I was feeling guilty because I had an argument with Verrick last night, but I didn't know that I'd hurt him so badly until you said you could smell his despair. That's all!"

"An argument? What about?"

I don't want to tell her. It's deeply personal and I still don't know how I feel about the whole thing. But I also don't want her to misunderstand things further. "We argued about Claiming, alright?" I burst out. "It's none of your concern! It has no bearing on where he is now. Every instant you waste with me is another minute that you could be actually looking for him!" I am practically yelling, but I don't care. Something is telling me that no matter how I am trying to comfort myself, Verrick is in grave danger.

"We both know who took him," I say. "You were apprised of the plan. The Cabal must have moved early and took Verrick without coming to me first so that I could switch out their sleeping potion. If they have him, they are going to kill him. We have to find him before they do!"

"I will find him," Friza responds coldly. "And make no mistake, if my Warchief dies, I will blame you. You say that the Cabal didn't come to you so you could switch the potions, but I only have your word that they didn't. This could have been a double-cross all along, with you working for the Cabal, but making us think you were on our side. One can never trust a spy."

I am frustrated beyond belief. We are going in circles, Friza and I. And wasting time. "I am not a spy," I say the words slowly, so that she cannot misunderstand me and can smell that I am telling the truth. "I have never done anything like this before.

I merely pretended to work with the Cabal so that we could capture them. Why would I want to hurt Verrick or help the Cabal? Doing so would only hurt my queen and Adrik in the long run. I am as loyal to my friend and country as you are to yours."

Friza still looks at me with a hardness in her eyes, but I can see that she is not as convinced of my guilt as she was before. Her body language changes ever so slightly, her confidence becoming questioning.

"But why would the Cabal move early, without your involvement? That part makes no sense."

I shake my head. "I don't know. Maybe they suspect I am not truly with them . . . in which case Verrick is in even more trouble than before. They will surely punish him for my betrayal."

"Even if you aren't lying," Friza responds, "if something happens to my Warchief, it will still be your fault. It was your plan that brought us to the south, to Grimblton. It is you that has gotten him captured, whether you wielded the poison used to take him or not."

Her words spear me inside and I feel pain unlike anything that I have felt before. Regret, guilt, sorrow, even a splash of rage, all mixing together as I absorb the blow of her condemnation. She's right. It was my plan that brought us here, that put Verrick in the role of bait, and in danger. If he dies . . . I will be to blame.

"I . . ." I say, at a loss for words, "I . . ."

At that moment, the dungeon door swings open, creaking and rasping on its old rusted hinges. I hear footsteps coming down the hallway and then an orc I don't know comes into my field of vision.

"Friza," he says, "we found something."

"What is it?" she asks eagerly. Turning away from me and heading to meet the other orc. Neither of them takes care lowering their voices, obviously not caring if I overhear them.

"Some broken glass under the bed," the orc says, pulling some shards from a satchel at his belt, showing them to Friza. "The scent is very faint but . . ."

". . . it smells like sleep potion." Friza finishes, having

smelled the glass herself. "It may have been gaseous in form, which explains the faint scent and the broken glass. They threw it into the room, probably while he was sleeping, and the gas knocked him out. But if they carried him from the room, we would still be able to follow his scent . . . unless . . ."

Friza turns to me. "Regent, you told Verrick that the Cabal contacted you from a secret chamber in the castles at High Citadel, correct?"

"Yes," I answer. " I never saw what they looked like."

"If there are secret ways in the castle at the capital that the Cabal used and knew about, then there could be secret ways in this castle as well. Quick, we must search the room and find the passageway where they took Verrick. We'll tear the room apart brick by brick if we have to!"

They get ready to leave when the orcress turns back to look at me.

"You will stay here," Friza orders, as if I have any choice other than to obey. "I am not done with you yet. The interrogation will continue when I return."

"But I can help!"

"You can help by remaining where I know I can find you," the orcress says coldly. "I'm still not completely convinced of your innocence in this matter. You were the one that brought us to the castle and put Verrick in that room. You could still be working with the enemy."

With that, she and the other orc leave, the dungeon door slamming shut with a resounding *boom*. Then I am alone with my thoughts. My feelings are all jumbled and snarled together that I hardly know what to think. There is my conversation with Korovi, my feelings for Verrick, Friza's distrust and Verrick's disappearance.

Is he already dead? Tortured? Though I still do not know what to call my feelings for Verrick, the thought of the world without him . . . it grows a pit of hopelessness and despair in me unlike anything I have ever felt. What if this feeling means that . . . I love him? The way Korovi described love? What if

Verrick is dead and not only did I not get to tell him, but he died thinking that I rejected him, that I didn't want him? Maybe even thinking like Friza, that I was the one that betrayed him? That thought is unbearable and I actually gasp in pain, my heart constricting.

So distracted am I by my thoughts that I almost don't hear a soft rumbling sound. I turn and look as far as I can beyond the bars, down the hallway and see part of the wall has opened up and out steps the mage, Hoggins.

"Hoggins?" I ask, bewildered. What is he doing stepping out of a secret passageway? So soon after Friza hypothesized their very existence? "What are you doing here?"

"I am sent to fetch you," he says simply, walking briskly toward my cell. He puts out his hand toward the lock. There's a stirring of the air, and then a popping sound as he sends a sharp burst of air into the mechanism, destroying the inner workings. The door swings open.

"Quickly, my lady. We must go before the orcs come back. The Cabal is waiting."

The Cabal? "Then you are . . ."

"Sting, yes. That is my name among my brothers and sisters. But we don't have time for this. Quick, to the passage."

I hesitate only for a brief second before following him. Wherever he is taking me, it will be closer to Verrick. Perhaps I will be able to free him or send a signal to Friza to rescue us. All things I can only do by heading deeper into the belly of the beast. So I leave my cell and plunge into the darkness of the secret passageway, the stone door rumbling closed behind me as I step in.

I am in total darkness.

"Take my hand," whispers Hoggins. "I will lead you where we need to go."

Reluctantly, I touch his hand. His grip is cool and clammy, a disconcerting combination. Like a corpse. But I keep my hand in his and let him lead through the corridors and up some stairs, all in pitch blackness.

"How did you know where to find me?"

"I am the Listener of the Cabal. I hear whispers everywhere. When I got to town to look for you, all anyone could talk about was that the orcs had taken you. I got back to the castle as quickly as I could and the servants said that they had thrown you to the dungeons. Why did they suspect you in the disappearance of their chief?"

Because you moved early, I think to myself. Aloud, I say, "I had an argument with Verrick last night."

"I know," he interrupts. "I heard it all. I cannot blame you for being so disgusted when he said he wanted to make you his mate, though it would have been wiser for our plan if you had played along. Though no harm done—we got him in the end."

He heard it *all*? Then he was there in another secret passage listening to Verrick and me as we . . . oh, I feel sick and violated. But I can't let him know that. "Yes, well, I was shocked. I reacted poorly, I admit. But anyway, the orcs smelled the remnants of the fight with their noses . . ."

Hoggins shudders in the dark. "Orcs are so unnatural, smelling their way around like beasts. Disgusting."

"Yes," I agree to placate him. "But when they couldn't find their Warchief and smelled the remnants of a fight, they assumed I had something to do with his disappearance. Why didn't you wait for me to administer the sleeping draught, like we discussed?"

"We didn't consider that the orcs might suspect you. I merely saw an opportunity when he was sleeping all alone to drug and take him. A quick throw of a potion and then we could secret him through the hidden passages. It was cleaner that way, rather than trying to catch you alone to give you the potion and instructions, and it allowed us to put our plan into effect quicker. Lord Agony will not like that you were treated so poorly, though." Hoggins says this last part as if to himself.

So Friza was right. They were listening and threw the sleeping gas into the room after I left and Verrick went to sleep. She was right as well about the passage in the room. By the time she finally finds the door in the other chamber, though, it will probably be too late. I need to keep following Hoggins so that I can find my lover.

Aloud, I ask, "Lord Agony?"

"Our leader. The one that brought you into this mission. You will meet him soon. He wants to see you before the ritual."

"The ritual?"

Hoggins coughs a little. "Ah, yes. You are not aware of our full plan. I only told you what you needed to know. But you have proven your loyalty and you are being rewarded by being brought to witness something amazing. Astonishing, even. You should be grateful. Ah, here we are. Just a moment . . ."

A clicking sound echoes in the small space around us and a door opens, the light outside blinding after so long in darkness, even though it is the dimmer light of sunset. The secret door opens into the gardens behind the castle, the hedge maze to be precise. Hoggins lets go of my hand as if holding it was as unpleasant for him as it was for me.

"Come," he says. "We must hurry to the tower before anyone sees us."

The tower? There is no tower behind Castle Grimble, but I don't have time to ask as he immediately starts walking. I have to jog slightly to keep up, my shorter legs no match for his stride. Left and right we turn, careening through the maze. I am all turned around, but Hoggins walks with the confident surety of one who has tread this path many times before. We navigate the maze until we come to a large artificial pond in the middle, fountain geysers spraying up in artful ways on the water. Hoggins steps onto the pond, walking on the water, two, three steps before disappearing. The pond must be an illusion.

Slowly, with a bit of unsureness in my steps, I step on the water where the mage did. It feels solid beneath my feet. With more assurance, I take my next steps until I feel myself pass through the cool mist of a magic illusion and find myself staring up at a vast tower, one that was not visible at all on the other side of the mirage. No wonder Friza and the other orcs cannot find where they took Verrick if there are so many secret, concealed places all over the castle. Hoggins stands at a doorway, looking back at me with impatience in his eyes.

"Hurry, we must get there before the sun completely sets."

Lifting my skirts a little, I walk up to the tower and through the door. Once inside, I see it is mainly hollow, with a huge spiral staircase that leads both upward and downwards. I peer downwards, but it is too dark to see where it leads. Hoggins walks up the stairs and I hurry to keep apace with him. Up, up we go, going up what must be hundreds of stairs until we finally reach a set of double doors at the very top of the tower. The doors open and I almost gag. The smell of something rotten mixes with the smell of blood in a truly horrifying and putrid way. I look and see the entire circular chamber is covered in blood, drawn in runes and lines on the walls and floor.

Gods, what kind of ritual can they be planning to hold? The amount of blood used . . . they must have killed several people to get enough.

A group of hooded and cloaked figures line the walls, all wearing different golden masks. On the opposite side of the ritual chamber is a throne, an exact replica of Yorian's throne at High Citadel, a vain, glittering thing of gold covered in gems. Sitting indolently on it is another masked figure, this one with the mask of a raven covering the upper part of his face. When he sees me, he rises, crossing the room with what I can only describe as boyish enthusiasm.

"Pells!"

Only one person calls me Pells, gods preserve me. The figure pulls back his hood and takes off his mask. There, standing amidst the blood and chaos, is Antony, Duke Strand.

He smiles wickedly, the expression threatening on his handsome face, and says, "Surprise."

CHAPTER 22

Pellia

"**A**ntony?" I ask, a little aghast. "You are the one that sent me the message from Yorian? You are the one that wants to expel the orcs from Adrik?"

Antony takes my hand in his and presses a kiss on the back of it. Seeing him do so, in this room reeking of rot and death, I have to stop myself from ripping my hand from his. My skin is crawling with his touch. But I have to be smart. I'm surrounded by enemies and I still don't know where Verrick is. I need to stay in their good graces until a chance presents itself to escape or summon help. So instead, I smile my prettiest, most winsome smile as Antony raises his lips and says, "I know this is a lot for you to absorb right now. You must have many questions. But yes, it was me sending you messages through Sting."

"Yes, I must confess, I am confused," I say, trying to look wide-eyed and innocent, looking around the room. "Where are we? What is this place? Why did you summon me?"

Antony chuckles condescendingly. "One thing at a time, my dear. One thing at a time. We are in the secret sanctum of the Cabal, an ancient organization that worships Grazrath, Lord of Pain. He offers us protection and prosperity in exchange for our service. As to why I summoned you. . . I thought you would like to see what your handiwork has wrought firsthand."

"My handiwork?"

"Yes, Pells, your handiwork. You brought the orc regent here, where we needed him, so that we may sacrifice him. After you were forced to seduce the beast—an offering, I assure you the Cabal appreciates—I thought that you would like to see his end and the beginning of a new regime."

My blood runs cold as he says the word "sacrifice," but I keep myself calm. If he wanted me to be present for the sacrifice, it means they haven't killed Verrick yet. My voice is steady as I ask, "A new regime? How can the death of one orc bring about such a thing?"

"This group has more power than you can imagine, Pells. You must know that this group was led by Yorian, from before he was even king. It was the backing of this group and Lord Grazrath that led to him becoming king instead of me. If only I had known about this group sooner, instead of Yorian! But no matter. With him gone, I am the inheritor of Yorian's will and the true heir to his throne. I am the Raven, harbinger of death and Lord Agony, leader of the Cabal. Soon, I will have the strength of Lord Grazrath and be king of this country. We will be free of orcish influence and you, my dear Pells . . . will be my queen."

His words are insane. They sound like the rantings of a madman. Perhaps he has been mad all along. Pretending to be flattered, I raise my brows and say, "Me? Your queen? You want me? Antony, I had no idea that you felt that way about me still." In truth, I didn't think that Antony ever had any feelings for me. I always felt it was merely a battle of wills between two rivals, with me as the prize he and Yorian fought over. That he was harboring an obsession to the point where he wants to take me as his queen . . . well, honestly I am surprised. And more than a little disturbed.

Antony steps closer, still holding my hand, looking fierce, a wild, possessive light in his eyes. 'My dear Pells, of course! I love you! It was always you. You were meant to be the queen of this country. It was Yorian's greatest mistake to put you aside for that traitorous, lowborn fairy bitch. With you at his side he would have been unstoppable. But now you will be *mine*, instead. As you were always meant to be."

The skin-crawling feeling comes back to me again, alarm spreading through me. I struggle to keep it off my face. But through sheer will, I keep my smile in place. It is the second declaration of love that I have received in the same number of days, but how different I feel about this one compared to Verrick's! I was panicked, to be sure, when Verrick spoke, but I felt safe to tell him what I truly thought. With this, I can see the ownership in Antony's eyes as he looks at me, and hear the lie in his words when he says he loves me. All things that were absent when Verrick, in his sincere, solemn way, told me his feelings. Oh, how could I have been so blind? I have to save him.

To that end, I bring my other hand up to clasp Antony's with both of my hands, in a way that I hope looks romantic. "Oh, Antony," I say, fluttering my lashes and looking demure, "my dearest friend. How happy I am to hear you say these things! I hope it's never been a secret that I always have had certain . . . feelings for you, even as I wasn't allowed to express them. We have been kept apart for too long!"

"Yes!" exclaims Antony, his eyes taking on a feverish, mad sort of gleam. "I knew you felt it too! Yorian kept us apart. But no longer! We were meant to be, you and I. You will sit by my side, my equal. We will rule this country and the Cabal in equal measure."

Then he kisses me. I fight back my shudder of revulsion, kissing him back with as much pretend passion as I can muster. His tongue shoves into my mouth, lukewarm and overly wet. It's absolutely disgusting, but I let out a fake moan. He pulls me into his arms and I fear he will try to go farther, when we are interrupted by a clearing of the throat.

We pull apart and Antony, with frustration in his features, barks out, "What?"

"Forgive me, sire," Hoggins, or I suppose Sting, says, "but the sun is about to set. If we are to do the ritual, it must be right now."

"Fine, fine," Antony sighs, pulling, thankfully, apart from me. "We will begin. Bring the sacrifice."

He gives me a look that is full of lust and mania. "We will continue this. Later. After we have completed the ritual."

His words sound like threats to my ears, but I give him a sultry smile before asking, "What is this ritual I keep hearing about? Why are we in your sanctum, and what are all these runes?"

He smiles and pulls me along, taking me through the bloody room to the throne. "I told you we needed a sacrifice, the blood of an enemy. It is for a ritual I found in our ancient texts. A way to summon the full strength of Lord Grazrath into my body. I will become stronger than a hundred orcs and be able to expel them from the country. Then we will invade Orik, this time with the backing of the strongest demon of the Nether, and take their foul country and kill the traitor queen and that animal she calls a husband."

"If there is such a ritual, why didn't Yorian use it before he invaded Orik the first time?"

Antony scoffs. "Because he was too weak and afraid to use it. The texts call it forbidden and warn against its use, but the ancestors were cowards! That much power, there for the taking and they left it sitting there. No, *I* am the one destined to wield Lord Grazrath's power. I will be his avatar and champion, because I have the ambition and will to do so."

He sits on the throne, dragging me with him so that I am sitting on his lap like a common harlot at a tavern. The hooded figures that surround the room make no move to look at us, but I still feel a little humiliated. Still, I smile and put my arms around him, as if there was no other place I would rather be.

"Kiss me again, Pells," he orders. "Let me feel how much you want me."

With little recourse, I lean down and kiss him. I'd almost forgotten the feeling of being forced to give affection to someone that I don't want. It is violating in a way that is hard to put into words. Being here with Antony reminds me of when I was with

Yorian, when I had to play the perfect, loving mistress to a man I despised. Luckily, I know how to give a practiced kiss, make the right noises and move my body just so, so that the man holding me doesn't know what I truly think of him.

I am using all my practiced arts on Antony when the door to the sanctum opens again. Antony pulls away from me and peers around my shoulder, a cruel smile growing on his face.

"Ah, the orc. Here at last."

I turn on Antony's lap, careful not to appear too eager. What I see makes my heart stop. Verrick, in thick, black chains, being pulled along by Sting and another Cabal member. The chains look strong, too strong to escape from. He looks at me sitting on Antony's lap, his face inscrutable. What must he think of me, sitting here with his enemy, after being captured when I swore he would be safe? Does he think me a traitor, like Friza? It is impossible to tell.

Antony's hands snake around my waist, holding me in a possessive grip when he says, "Look at him. It must destroy him to see that you are truly mine. Did you know, Pells, that he was concerned about you? He must have developed feelings for you, like the oaf he is. Sting, did you not hear him ask to make Pells his mate?"

"I did, sire."

"And what did she say?"

Sting says in an uninterested tone, "She refused him and was disgusted, of course. As any true human woman would be."

The man holding me laughs, a spiteful sound, "You did your job too well, Pells. Did you have anything you wish to say to this pathetic creature before he meets his end?"

I think fast, faster than I ever have in my life. What can I do? What can I say? How can I turn this situation to my advantage so that I can save Verrick and we can both escape?

Finally, I laugh, a mirror to Antony's, letting cruelty drip from my voice as I say, "I have nothing to say to that stupid beast. He should have known that no human could truly have feelings for him. No, I have nothing to say to him. But I do have a request for you, dear Antony."

"What is it, Pells?"

I take a deep breath, smile and say, "When it is the time in the ritual to kill him? Please, Antony. Let me do it."

CHAPTER 23

Verrick

The human man who holds Pellia laughs, his hands digging into her sides like claws. "I knew you were perfect! Heartless and bloodthirsty, my exact equal."

Pellia titters, but I can tell it is an act. Each time the man touches her pheromones spike, causing the smell of revulsion to roll off of her in waves. But she sits on him with practiced ease, leaning into his grip. Without the nose of an orc, it would be impossible to tell what she is truly thinking. She says, "I want to punish him for every time I was forced to endure his touch. To take my own vengeance against the orcs. For me and for Yorian. Please, Antony, let me be the one to do it."

Her eyes slide over to me, and I can smell her guilt over her words. I wish she wouldn't feel so conflicted. I don't care what she says, as long as she masks her true feelings and survives. She has forgotten that I can smell her every emotion since she obviously has not had her *orikiri* tea this morning. Everything she is thinking is clear in her scent. She is playing a dangerous game. I can tell that she is trying to put together some sort of plan, though I can't tell what she truly wants. But she is manipulating the human lord for some end. Nervousness spikes in her scent, though her smile never slips. Her hands come up and stroke the male's chest, a teasing caress I have experienced, but it never looked so rehearsed. The human doesn't seem to notice, though.

His hands come up and take hers, replying, "While I would love to see you with blood on your hands, unfortunately, the ritual requires me to drain him myself. It is how the ritual ends, binding Lord Grazrath's strength into my body permanently. I must drink from him like a vampire, take the power of my enemy inside myself."

"Then let me help," insists Pellia. She strokes his face and places a lingering kiss on his lips. "I will hold the blade that you will use and give it to you when the time comes."

Antony gives her a considering look, and for a moment, everything seems to freeze. The last light of the setting sun pierces into the room, illuminating the throne where he sits with Pellia. Has he realized that she is trying to use him? Has she overplayed her hand? Will they hurt her? My sluggish limbs tense in their cursed bonds and, for a second, I feel like strength is returning to me, as if I could burst out of my confines to protect my love if need be. Then the man laughs and gives Pellia another kiss. Another wave of disgust rolls off of her and then he says, "Alright, Pells. So be it. I never could really say no to you—besides, our Cabal owes you for your sacrifice of having to take this creature to bed. You will stand beside me as we complete the ritual and hold the knife. An honor, to be sure."

"Oh, thank you Antony," she smiles, and then pulls herself off of his lap. "You said the ritual had to take place at sunset? Shall we begin?"

The human male laughs again, sounding manic. "So impatient, Pells. But you are right. Sting!"

The skull-masked human next to me starts. "Yes, sire?"

"Bring me the sacrificial knife. Pellia will be my assistant for the ritual."

Sting tenses next to me, smelling affronted. I wonder if he was meant to have the honor of assisting Antony before Pellia intervened. But aloud he says, "Of course, sire. Here it is."

He pulls out a wicked-looking blade with a gold hilt and a long, jagged edge. It smells of dark magic and death and has

obviously been used many times before. Sting carries the
over to Pellia, who takes it with gravity. She shares a cruel smile
with Antony and looks at me with cruel intent on her features,
even as worry spikes in her scent. What is she planning? I want
to tell her not to worry about freeing me, but to worry about her
own escape, but I know I can't say anything without giving away
her game. Her eyes dart to Antony, who steps forward, standing
in the center of the room, at the nexus of all the bloody lines
and runes the cover every inch of the chamber's surfaces. Pellia's
hand grips the knife and I suddenly get the feeling that she is
going to attack Antony with the knife. My muscles tense, weak
as they are. When she moves, I'll launch myself forward to create
a distraction. Hopefully she times it just right, or she'll fail and
we'll both be dead.

"Brothers! Sisters!" exclaims the human male, pulling his
raven mask back onto his face. "Intone the chant! It is time!"

Dark speech fills the chamber, the hooded figures
beginning a chant from around the room. The lines and runes
on the walls and floor start to glow with sinister red light.
Pellia's eyes go wide, even as she steps forward, standing next to
Antony. The air grows heavy and thick; the room darkening as
the last light of the sun dips below the horizon, leaving us in the
shadows of night.

Antony lifts his hands up above his head and chants along
with his followers. I am no student of cursed languages, but I
can tell they speak in the tongue of demons and catch the word
"Grazrath" several times. The ritual continues as the hooded
figures along the walls lift their hands as well, making an "x"
with their arms above their heads. The glowing runes become
more intense and Antony in the center of the room rises in the
air, the red glow encasing him.

He shouts a triumphant laugh, "It's working! It's working,
Pells! I can feel the power . . . my soul is opening, receiving the
boon of Grazrath!"

"That's amazing Antony!"

Pellia steps forward, closer to Antony, her grip tightening

on the knife in her hands. She is standing behind him and I can feel her intent. She's going to stab him before the ritual can proceed further. I try to catch her eye, to communicate that this isn't the time, that if she spills blood in the middle of such a dark ritual, there could be untold consequences, but I can't get her attention without pulling the room's attention to her and her slowly rising blade.

Then a pulse of power rockets through the room, centered on Antony. Pellia is pushed back, almost losing her footing. At that moment, Antony flies up higher in the room, his body pulsing with dark energy. His triumphant laughter chokes off and he suddenly says, "Wait, something . . . something is not right . . . stop! Stop!"

But it appears to be too late, his body bowing backwards at an unnatural angle. He screams, a high-pitched, inhuman sound, then wings, huge and batlike rip out of his back. The chanting stops as the room looks at him in horror, his shrieks rending through the air. His hands reach back and feel the wings, moving with panicked haste as black claws suddenly erupt from his fingers. His new talons rip into his flesh and he twists and writhes in the air, when horns burst from his forehead, twisting up into the air like mountain spires. The dark red power continues to pulse through the room, when his screams suddenly cut off and his body falls through the air. He lands in a heap on the floor, the runes still glowing malevolently.

Sting steps toward him, hesitantly reaching out a hand. "Sire? Are you well?"

Pellia stands behind him, knife still in hand. Her eyes finally find mine and we look at each other. I keep my face unreadable, but I try to tell her with my gaze to run. To leave this place. Whatever is happening is dark, foul magic and we are all in danger. She must see something in my eyes, because she steps back, one step, then two.

Deep, disjointed laughter grows from the heap in the middle of the room. The figure of Antony rises, pulling himself to his feet, showing that he is now at least a foot taller than he was. Claw-tipped fingers come up and rip the raven mask off of his face, even as the laughter grows, a distorted, inhuman sound.

"At last," the monstrous figure says, his voice an unnaturally low bass. "At last I am free from the Nether. I am free from my fetid prison and my thirst can finally be slaked!"

He looks up, his skin pulled taut across his bones, pale with black veins showing through. His eyes pierce through the dark, yellow and red with a snake's thin pupil.

"At last!" he shouts, "Lord Grazrath is free!"

CHAPTER 24

Pellia

Lord Grazrath, in Antony's body, laughs, a horrible aberrant sound. "Well? Bow to your lord, Cabal of Grazrath. For I have returned! Show how glad you are to serve me!"

The cloaked and hooded figures around the demon lord murmur, an air of fear in the room. I can almost make out what they are saying. They meant to summon the strength of Grazrath, not Grazrath himself. But self-preservation is a powerful force and within moments the Cabal all bows, groveling before the demon lord. Keeping the knife firmly in my hand, I join them, sinking into a deep curtsey, though I keep my eyes on the demon in front of me.

"Hail, Grazrath, Lord of Pain," intones one figure.

"Hail," echoes the rest.

Grazrath looks over the gathered crowd, a sneer on his possessed lips. "Ah," he says, "My Cabal. You have been faithfully serving me for many years. The pain and death you dedicated to me fed me in my captivity."

"It heartens us to hear our service was useful," replies the same figure that spoke before.

"Your service was nothing compared to what we will do now that I am free," the demon replies, using Antony's distorted mouth.

"Ah, my lord . . ." begins Sting, still deep in a servile crouch.

"Is Lord Antony in there with you? Are you as one or . . ?"

"Worried about your dear leader? You should be—he has taken my place in the Nether with the death goddess Karnia and all my trapped demonic brothers and sisters. His sacrifice is . . .appreciated."

"His sacrifice is appreciated," murmurs the cultists around the room, repeating the demon lord. Obviously, they don't know what to do and so are following the creature they summoned, hoping to not enrage him. It is like being locked in a room with a rabid wolf. The only thing to do is appease it and hope that it doesn't turn on you.

The demon lord steps forward, out of the center of the room and says, "But the ritual is not complete yet, is it? I must drink the blood of an enemy and seal my place in this body. Before it falls apart." His taloned hands come up and feel his face, as if suddenly aware that Antony's body is being torn apart by his presence within it.

"Where is the enemy that I must drain?"

"Here, my Lord Grazrath," says the hooded figure that is still standing next to Verrick. He takes the black chains that bind Verrick and shakes them.

"Ah, yes. The orc regent. I've heard of you through the prayers of my followers. They cursed you and your kind and asked that I eradicate them. I suppose I must, in order to complete the ritual. But your thoughts are not of yourself or your own doom . . . you worry about the safety of . . ."

He turns and seemingly sees me for the first time. A cruel smile twists his stolen lips.

"You," Lord Grazrath says, pointing directly at me, "come closer."

Sting, hurrying at my side, grabs me with an iron grip, and pushes me toward the contorted visage of my once-childhood friend. But I don't resist. What point would there be? I'm being pulled toward the Lord of Pain and Shadow, an archdemon. I'm sure he could catch me if I ran. Besides, I still need to figure out a way to save Verrick as well as myself. From the corner of my eye I see the orc warchief struggling against his bonds, a burning look in his eyes. Cursing me? I can't tell. But for all intents and purposes, I must look like I've betrayed him. From my performance with Antony, and now my seeming worship of a demon.

I can't think of that right now. Instead, I let Sting pull me and when I arrive at the bottom of the dais, yank away from his grip, just so that I sink into a low curtsey, tilting so that I know my cleavage is on advantageous display. I figure it can't hurt.

"My lord Grazrath," I say, trying to imbue my tone with the worshipfulness the demon lord probably expects.

"Stand," he orders carelessly, his voice like nails against slate in my mind. When I obey, he lazily twirls a finger around, the tips of his stolen body's fingers a dead black around his talons. "Spin for me."

Warily, I turn, trying and failing to understand what is happening. When I'm done, Lord Grazrath leans back, the picture of arrogance, and looks at me with an indolent eye. "You are the woman both this body and that orc are obsessed with, are you not?"

I curtsey again. "Yes, Antony had some tender feelings for me, sire. The orc, I could not say." I want to get his focus off of Verrick as much as I can.

The demon laughs, the sound like cruel thunder, before replying, "Whatever feelings this body had for you, tender is not how I would describe them. The orc though . . . he is desperate for your safety, even though you have betrayed him."

He looks at me, as if gauging my worth, then says, "Very well. In recognition of the service this body has done to me, I will make you my first pleasure pet. You will kneel at my feet and wait on my whim."

Still in my curtsey, I say, "You honor me, my Lord Grazrath." A roil of disgust moves through me and the demon smiles, twisting Antony's face into something not quite human.

"Your feelings do not match your words, pet," he observes as he grins. "No matter. You'll serve anyway."

He walks past me, even as I am still sunk into my curtsey. Behind me I hear him sit on the throne that Antony was so lately lounging on. How things can change in just a matter of moments.

"Come here, pet. I have a few moments before I must drain the orc. I rather like that thought of him going to the Nether with the image of you servicing me burned into his mind first."

Slowly, I rise from my curtsey and turn around. I smile, even though I know he can read at least surface thoughts and thus will know my smile is not real. I don't think he will care, though. Males of power seldom care whether you actually enjoy servicing them. They just want the appearance of enjoyment. With a demon of pain, perhaps he even takes perverse pleasure in my disgust and helplessness.

"But of course, Lord Grazrath. I live to serve," I say, walking carefully toward the hideous demon. His human skin is stretched too tightly over the overgrown bones of his transformation. His wings are too big, dwarfing the throne behind him, and his smile is stretched too wide, like a horrifying mask of flesh. He really looks like his body is falling apart. I can see why he needs to finish the ritual. But leave it to a sadistic monster to want to mentally torture Verrick before killing him.

I can't think of my plan too much. I don't know how many of my thoughts he can sense, so I move purely on instinct. Kneeling in front of him, I smile like it's carved on my face in stone. All I know is I can't let him hurt Verrick.

So I keep smiling, even as he opens his robe, displaying his turgid member. It's purple and bulbous in a strange way, no longer quite human, just like the rest of Antony's body.

"Suck," he commands, his obvious pleasure in the command cruel.

I lean closer, lowering my lids halfway to give a seductive gaze. I don't know why I'm bothering. It's plain that he desires my pain and discomfort more than anything. He's using me to torture my lover before killing him and maybe even tormenting what might be left of Antony in his head.

I open my mouth and right before I can put his disgusting cock in my mouth, my left hand tightens on the sacrificial dagger that I am still holding. No one noticed it, probably underestimating me because I am female and seeing no danger from my quarter. With all the strength I possess, I stab him deep in the join between his pelvis and leg and yank, pulling the blade through his putrid cock. An unholy shriek rends the air and Lord Grazrath backhands me, sending me flying down the steps. Behind me, I hear a roar and I think it might be Verrick, but I am too befuddled to tell.

Lord Grazrath launches himself down from the throne, landing on top of me, blood pouring from his pelvis. I feel the warm wetness of the blood spill onto me and my dress.

"You stupid cunt!" seethes the demon. "I was going to let you live, as long as you served me on your knees, with your mouth and cunt and blood! But you dare attack me? Me? Lord of Pain and Misery?"

One of his hands shoots out, grasping my throat and squeezing. My hand still holds the dagger and with what little energy I have left, I slash the dagger with all my might toward his arm. But his other hand catches my wrist and squeezes, breaking the bones, and the knife falls from my limp hand. A scream tries to leave my throat, but he is squeezing too tightly. All that comes out is a weak rasp.

My vision is covered in white spots and then darkens around the edges. My last thought is, *So this is how I die, killed by a demon while trying to save my lover.*

Then it all goes black.

CHAPTER 25

Verrick

My heart stops as Pellia flies through the air, landing heavily on the glowing stone floor. As she lands, I roar, pulling at my bonds, only to be yanked back by my puny captor. Cursed human. There's no way he could control me so easily if I were not weakened by the Hex Chains surrounding me.

As it is, I am helpless as Lord Grazrath launches from his throne, flying and landing directly on the body of my beloved. His cock dangles from his body, barely held on by a thin piece of skin. Pellia has essentially castrated a demon with the power of a god. Not only that, but she seems to have severed the artery leading from the pelvis to the leg. Blood pumps from the wound, but the demon is still standing. Even in his mortal shell, he must have some access to his immortal power. He would be dying from Pellia's blow otherwise.

"You stupid cunt!" seethes the demon. "I was going to let you live, as long as you served me on your knees, with your mouth and cunt and blood! But you dare attack me? Me? Lord of Pain and Misery?"

His hand shoots out and begins choking the life out of Pellia. The woman I love. She bucks and flails under him, her hand with the dagger coming up to slash him again, but his other hand shoots out with preternatural speed. His grip constricts and I can see her delicate bones shatter under his attack. A horrible, pained gasp leaves her lips and then her hand falls to the ground. Her body completely slackens and her eyes roll into the back of her head, even as the skin of her face purples.

The demon laughs again. "Die, bitch, die!" Then he finally pulls his hand away from her throat and Pellia doesn't move, still as death.

Something breaks within me. I stare at the body of the woman I have learned to love more than life itself and anguish unlike anything I've ever experienced tears through me.

A sound unlike anything I've ever made erupts from my throat. A sound of pain and loss and fury. It blends together, getting higher and louder until the screams of the surrounding cultists join in, the hooded figures clutching their heads and thrashing about in pain.

Even the unholy figure of Lord Grazrath is affected by the sound, his hands coming up to his ears even as he rears back from Pellia's prone form. He whirls toward me and snarls, "Siren-born!"

He lunges forward, but the scream coming from my mouth just gets louder and all the windows of the chamber shatter at once, spraying glass outward. The cultists drop one by one, their screams still twined with mine, even as their strength leaves them.

It strikes me that I am death screaming, something I thought I was incapable of. But seeing Pellia killed in front of me has snapped something deep within me, accessing a well of pain that I didn't know existed. The death scream intensifies and I feel the chains around me weaken, as if the metal itself is growing brittle at the sound.

Blood drips from the corner of Lord Grazrath's eyes, his hands still pressed firmly on his ears. He looks at his dying followers all around him. Finally, he growls, "You'll regret this, siren-born!" before jumping out of one of the broken windows, his huge wings snapping open and flying away into the darkness.

The screams of the hooded figures on the ground go silent

one by one and I have the thought that if Pellia is, by some miracle, still alive, I may be hurting her, killing her. I try to stop screaming, but I have lost control and I have no way of mastering this power inside me. As the last of the cultists go silent, I pull mightily at the chains. They break as if made of sandstone, falling off of my upper body and arms. Finally, finally, the scream seems to die down and with great effort, I force myself silent once again.

I launch myself forward, past all the bodies on the ground, blood pouring out of their eyes from behind their masks. Uncaring at the death all around me, I fall to my knees next to Pellia's body, my hands trembling as I reach out to her. A single tear of blood has fallen out from the corner of one of her eyes, perversely giving me hope. It means that she was still alive to be affected by my scream. I touch her neck and at first feel nothing. I press a little harder into her flesh and then feel it. A very, very faint pulse, coming from a weak but still living heart.

I have to get her out of here. She needs a healer immediately or she will fade. I can feel it. I gather her in my arms, though they are still weakened by being held in the Hex Chains for so long. But for all her curves, Pellia still feels light, a welcome burden for me to carry. I pick her up and hurry out of the ritual chamber, the runes still glowing behind me as I leave. I want to take my love out of this place of horrors and death as soon as possible.

I make my way carefully down the spiral staircase. I am getting winded just from moving, something that has never happened to me in my adult life. Never have I felt this fatigued even in the heat of long battles or after days of not sleeping on the march. But I suppose being drugged and cursed for so long has affected me greatly. None of that matters. I just need to get the precious person in my arms to safety.

After what seems like eternity, I descend to where the door is. Before, when they took me up from the dungeons, I was too weak to even try to escape through the door as they dragged me past it. Now, even tired and winded as I am, I kick up the door, watching with some satisfaction as it bursts open, the latch on the door breaking. We appear to be in the center of a pond of some sort and brace myself to go down into the water, but as I step forward, I find I am on solid ground. An illusion then. I race forward, finding myself in a hedge maze, and yell, "FRIZA! FRIZA!"

There's a shout in the distance, then I hear the sounds of chaos coming toward me.

I call out again, "FRIZA! BRING THE HEALER!"

There are crashing sounds, and then I see one of the hedges topple down to my left. Friza and a contingent of my orcs come running at me, axes in hand. There is no healer with them. I see that they have cut a swathe in the maze, creating a straight path out and toward the castle. I begin to run, pushing my weakened body to its limits, but I must, I *must* get Pellia to help while there is still time.

Friza comes towards me, but I run past her, running toward the castle. She begins jogging with me.

"Why are you running?" she demands. "Where in the Nether were you? I've had everyone looking for you and . . ."

"There's no time for that," I cut her off. "Where is the healer?"

"How would I know where the healer is? Are you hurt? I. . ." She trails off as if noticing for the first time who and what I carry.

"Gods! How is she with you? I left her in the dungeon."

"You did *what*?" I bark. We are finally out of the maze. I see some servants gathering, whispering to each other. I don't have time for this, nor time for Friza and her strange statements.

"You there!" I shout, for all the world sounding like the tyrant humans believe orcs to be. "Get the healer! NOW!"

The servants scatter and I turn to Friza. "I want the healer sent to my chamber now. Pellia will die if we do not get healing magic into her soon."

"She might have been the one that betrayed you and got you taken . . ." Friza protests.

"SHE WAS NOT!" I yell, not enjoying being countermanded

when so much is at stake. "She risked her life for me! She is dying because she tried to save me. Now, if I don't see the healer this instant, I will burn down this entire town until I find him!"

Friza only hesitates for an instant more before shouting out, "You heard the Warchief! Find the healer and bring him to the chamber! Move!"

For the first time, I notice that the orcs that came with Friza have been following us. They scatter like the servants, moving with more speed than the humans, running to find the healer. I would even take his blasted assistant at this point. Someone needs to work on bringing Pellia back. She is slipping through my fingers, even as I hold her tightly in my arms.

While the others run this way and that, I hurry into the castle and bring her to the chamber that we were in just last night, as it is the only room that has been prepared and isn't sitting under a fine layer of dust. When I enter, I gently, oh so gently, place Pellia's slack body on the bed. Fear grips my heart like never before. Not when the sirens wanted to kill me as a youth. Not when I found the clan treasures stolen by Lucy. Nothing compares to this moment as I stare down at this brave, delicate human, looking so small and unmoving.

Friza bursts into the room saying, "The healer's been found; he's on his way."

"He better be hurrying," I growl, rage building in as my helplessness grows. "If Pellia dies I will take it from his hide."

My second doesn't comment on my violence, only asks, "How did this happen? How was she there with you? Why is she so injured? We heard a horrific sound coming from the middle of the hedge maze and then . . ."

"It was my death scream," I say, not looking at her. I sit on the edge of the bed, taking Pellia's hand in mine. She feels so cold to the touch. I reach out to check her pulse. Still there, but weak, so very weak and stuttering. "Where is that thrice-damned healer?"

"Here! Here, Regent Verrick," says the man, bustling into the room. He takes one look at Pellia on the bed and makes the sign of the pantheon.

"My gods! Who would do this to the regent?"

"That isn't important. What's important is you bringing her back."

"Right," the healer says, all business. He steps forward and places his hand on her forehead. "Her spirit is still within, but very faint. I'll have to work fast. Oh, where is that bothersome assistant? She's never where I need her!"

"I'll find her," says Friza and exits the room. I hear some yelling as she goes, and I know I can count on my second to do what must be done.

Gently, but firmly, the healer says, "You'll need to leave as well, Regent Verrick. This is delicate work I do and I cannot risk being distracted."

"I will not leave her side."

"You will if you want her to live," he says, more firmly than before. "I will tell you the moment there is any change. But for now, I need privacy, save my assistant to shore up my powers. Please, go."

I cannot argue with him about it. My presence is doing more harm than good. So I quietly kiss her forehead and murmur, "Come back to me, Pellia. I'll never ask anything of you again if you will just come back to me." And with that, I leave the room.

I do not go far. I pace outside the chamber door. Listening with all my strength, trying to see if I can detect any change. If I hear anything amiss, I know I won't be able to stop myself from bursting through the door.

I could not say how long I paced before Friza returns with the assistant in tow. The half-elf woman disappears in the room and then I am alone with my second.

"You should rest," Friza declares in that blunt way of hers. "You look like shit."

"I will rest when I know she is better." I growl, though I know my friend is right. My limbs tremble even as I pace, but I feel like if I stop moving that I will collapse.

"At least tell me what happened," insists my second. "The last I knew you were missing, and the regent was in the dungeons. And did you say that you did a death scream?"

"Why was she in the dungeons?" I remember now, Friza saying something like that in the hedge maze.

"Because you were *missing*! Because we were here as a part of a plot I didn't fully understand at Regent Santir's orders and then you were gone? What was I to think? I thought she had double-crossed us and that you were in danger."

"I was in danger, but it wasn't because of Pellia. And where the fuck was Korovi? Why did he let you take her?"

Friza has the grace to look chagrined. "He didn't *let* us take her. He fought three orcs at the same time and was only taken down because the regent distracted him. I have him chained up in the healer's tent."

Though I am still distressed waiting for news of Pellia, I have a brief moment of amusement. "You were busy, weren't you?"

"You were gone! Taken! What would you have had me do?"

"Not throw my m . . . the regent into the dungeons. However, I suppose I can't fault your suspicion. Korovi will need to get a commendation after this, though." Perhaps I will petition for him to go to Garden Manor so that he can find a bride of his own.

Friza is unamused by my errant comments. "Stop dodging the question. Where were you? What happened? Why is the regent on death's door?"

The reminder of Pellia kills any other thoughts I might be having. I grimly respond, "I am not dodging the question. The Cabal took me to their secret tower to be ritually sacrificed."

My second makes a strangled sound of shock and protest, but I continue on. "The tower is hidden in the maze where you found me, cloaked under some sort of illusion. They meant to summon the strength of the demon lord they serve, but accidentally summoned the demon himself. He's the one who almost killed Pellia. When I saw it, helpless to stop it, as he squeezed the life out of her . . . the death scream came. I can't explain it and I am not sure I could do it again, but it came. I killed the rest of the cultists, but the demon fled."

"Gods! Which demon?"

"Grazrath, Lord of Pain."

Friza swears. "Those crazy bastards! They brought that depraved torturer into this realm? If half the stories about him are true . . ."

"I would believe them," I state grimly. Damn it, where is that healer? Why does he not come out of the room? Is there still no news?

"Then we should send scouts to find him, try to bind him before he can do more damage. Where is the mage?"

"Do not send any orcs looking for him. In fact, order all the orcs back to the castle," I command.

"Why?"

"They mentioned that they needed the blood of an enemy to seal the ritual. They didn't say that they specifically needed my blood, though I was the one they took. Still, I don't want to risk that the demon gets the blood he needs from another source. Without it, his body was already falling apart. I think that if he doesn't get orc blood before this night is over, he will be sent back to the Nether."

"Then we should at least send the human guards to search for him. They won't reach the criteria of an enemy, would they?"

"I don't know," I admit. "Maybe not. But if they are truly on our side, maybe they would. I think it would be best to leave it well enough alone until tomorrow. We can search for evidence that he still lives then. But maybe we should send some of the human guards to the tower where I was held. There is dead to burn there. I killed all of them with my scream. We should do it quickly since they died in such a cursed place. They could become undead."

"If you killed all the others, why didn't Pellia die, then?" asks Friza.

"I don't know. Maybe because she was unconscious when

it began, so she couldn't fully hear the scream, or perhaps already too far gone to be affected. Maybe a bored god mercifully intervened. I don't care, I only know that I need her to wake once again."

Friza nods and says, "Alright, I'll send them to gather the bodies. We'll burn them soon. We should be able to find the tower by following the trail of your scent." She clasps both hands to her chest and then turns to leave. Then she turns back and says, "I'm sorry, Warchief. I hope she lives." Then she is gone.

Me too, I think. *Life will not be worth living without her.*

✽ ✽ ✽

The light of morning is firmly in the sky when the healer comes out of the room. He looks wan and spent and for a moment I fear the worst. Then he smiles faintly and says the sweetest words I have ever heard, "She'll live."

Then everything goes black as I collapse.

CHAPTER 26

Pellia

Consciousness comes slowly back to me. The first thing I notice is that I am in no pain, though I feel heavy, like lead, my limbs not wanting to respond to my call to move. Have I died? Am I in the Nether? Am I about to be led to judgment by Lacrys, the death goddess Karnia's lover and steward?

Then my eyes finally open, and I see I am back in the room at Castle Grimble. The one from before my fight with Verrick. Was it all a dream? I feel confused, discombobulated, as if I have no anchor. I try to sit up, but a gentle hand pushes me down.

"No need for that right now, Regent," says a soft, feminine voice. "Take things slowly. You've been gone for quite some time."

I have? I turn my head slowly and see a round-cheeked woman in white robes at my side. Her skin is a dark tan, with black hair that is pulled back into a severe bun at her nape. Slightly pointed ears peek out from her hair, denoting her as a half-elf. She looks familiar, but I take a moment to place her.

"The healer's assistant," I croak out, my throat completely parched.

The woman nods and then pours water into a metal goblet. Her soothing hands come under my head, propping me up slightly so that I can drink. I draw the water in eagerly, but she admonishes, "Slowly, slowly. You don't want to be sick."

Chastened, I slow down, but still revel in the feeling of the liquid quenching my thirst and comforting my rasping throat.

When I have finally finished drinking, the healer's assistant lays me back down and puts the goblet on the bedside table. She then fixes my blankets with the brusk sort of care of one who has done the action many times before.

"I'll go tell the others you have finally awoken," says the woman, brushing some wrinkles out of the front of her robe. "They have all been eagerly awaiting you."

"How long was I asleep?" I ask, my voice sounding more natural, but still huskier than usual. I need more water.

"About a week," says the healer's assistant.

A week? The other woman must see the dismay on my face, because she says kindly, "You had much to heal from. You came to us at death's door. If my master were not as skilled with his magics and tonics as he is, then you would have never made it."

Death's door? Suddenly, the rest comes flooding back to me. The ritual. The demon. My desperate bid to kill him that failed and then his cruel hand at my throat, the crushing pressure and no air. What happened after that? How did I survive such an ordeal?

The healer's assistant answers my stunned silence by leaving the room. But I am not alone for long. The door bursts open and there is Verrick. Alive. Safe. Whole. I immediately blink back tears of relief.

"Verrick . . ." I say, then stop. What can I say? Sorry for breaking your heart and getting you captured early? Sorry I failed to rescue you? Please believe me, I never betrayed you? All those things sit at the tip of my tongue, but I say none of them.

Verrick doesn't seem to notice my turmoil, however, and merely leans down, taking me up into a crushing embrace.

"You came back," he is saying, relief and joy dripping off of his every word. "You came back."

Slowly, I take my hands up and embrace him as well. "Sorry I kept you waiting," I say, while holding him tight. Tears gather in my eyes again, and this time I can do nothing but let them fall.

He is not angry with me. He seems to understand.

Then an awkward *ahem* breaks into our moment and we pull apart to see the healer and the assistant standing in the doorway, watching us. I can't bring myself to feel embarrassed, however. I am too happy to see Verrick.

"I'll need to check on my patient," the healer says, coming forward. "How are you feeling, Regent Santir?"

To my dismay, Verrick pulls back from me as the healer speaks, moving out of the way so that the old man can examine me. Verrick hangs on the edges of the chamber, hovering just out of reach. Why is he so quick to leave me?

But they asked me a question. So I turn to the healer and say, "I'm feeling well. No lingering pain."

"Your throat?" he asks, putting a deft hand on my wrist to check my pulse. "Your wrist? Any stiffness or discomfort?"

For the first time, I think of Grazrath, bleeding on top of me, shattering my bones. I lift my right wrist and flex it. It's perfectly fine. The healer must have been working very hard on me indeed for a broken bone to be fixed so quickly.

"It feels as good as new," I assure the elderly man. "Thank you so much for your efforts."

The healer chuckles before taking my hand and closing his eyes. "I would not have dared do anything other than my best, my lady."

That's a strange thing to say, but before I can comment, I feel a rush of healing magic pour into my body. It is a gentle feeling, probing this way and that, as if searching for any aches and pains. After a moment, the healer releases my hand and says, "Everything seems good. Your soul was rather fraying at the edges for a while. You gave us quite the scare, my lady."

My *soul* was *fraying* at the edges? How close did I come to dying? Alarmed, I look at Verrick, who merely looks stoically back. After his initial outburst, he has withdrawn into his normal, severe self. Perhaps it is because we are in front of an audience. The thought makes me want to dismiss the healer and his assistant, but I also don't want to be rude. They have apparently saved my life, after all.

The healer continues, "I see no reason you cannot have visitors. I'll inform Her Majesty at once."

"You'll inform who?" My eyes bug out. Adalind is here? But the healer doesn't respond and simply leaves the room, his assistant trailing behind him. Then I am alone with Verrick.

I still don't know what to say to him. He has retreated from me more than physically. As I look at him, standing as far as he can from the bed I am laying in, he seems guarded suddenly. After all that we have been through, now he wants to stay away from me? I thought we were good when he first came in, but it seems the healer's visit has put distance between us. How do I fix this?

I begin, "Are you well? The Cabal didn't hurt you?"

"I am fine," he says, his voice almost oddly calm. It's impossible to tell what he is thinking.

I don't know what else to say, so I ask, "And Korovi? He is not too angry, is he? He got hurt because of me."

"So I heard," responds Verrick in that same tone. "He is fine. He was merely worried about you, as we all were."

Oh. Well, then. I suppose there's no more beating about the bush. I blurt out, "I'm sorry you were taken . . . it was my fault . . ."

"No, it wasn't," Verrick returns, his voice still even.

"It was! Hoggins told me . . . oh, gods! Hoggins! He's one of the Cabal! We should . . ."

"He's dead," Verrick says bluntly. "They all are. We burned them last week."

That brings me up short for a moment. Shocked, I ask, "All of them? Dead? But how? Did Grazrath . . ."

"No," interrupts Verrick, "I did. I *death screamed*."

"You *death screamed*? But . . . I thought you said that wasn't one of your gifts."

"It would appear that I am capable of it, when given the proper motivation," he answers cryptically. I suppose he means when his life is in danger. Useful, that.

"Then did you kill Grazrath, or rather Antony's body?"

"No," he replies. "I have bad news on that front. He escaped out the windows while the others were dying. I tried to keep him from finding any other orcs to drain to complete the ritual . . . but before they could be recalled to the castle, one of the scouts I had on the border of the town was found with puncture wounds and drained of blood. Runes were carved into his body with what appeared to be talons. We believe the demon succeeded and is at large. We could not find his trail though and have no idea where he is now."

Grave news, indeed. "I'm sorry that I failed when I tried to kill him."

"You keep apologizing," he says gruffly. "You have nothing to apologize for."

"But I looked like I betrayed you! You were taken early because of our argument and then when I was with Antony I said such vile things about you . . ."

"I could smell that you were not being truthful about the things you said. You didn't take your *orikiri* leaf tea, remember? I could clearly smell your intentions. You put yourself in the midst of a den of vipers and tried to rescue me, putting yourself in grave danger at the same time. How can you think you need to apologize for such bravery?"

His words leave me speechless. But if he knew I was playacting the whole time, why is he suddenly being distant? Could it be our argument? But that feels like it was so long ago . . . like a lifetime. So many things have happened since then. My feelings . . . well, they are still confused, but I know one thing: I want Verrick in my life and in my bed. I want to fall into him with all the relief that I have that we are both still alive.

But before I can say anything, the door bursts open and Queen Adalind enters the room.

"Pell!"

She gathers me into an embrace that I return easily. Adalind is one of my closest friends, the only one who truly understands what I went through with Yorian.

Behind Adalind, Verrick coughs and says, "I'll leave you two the room." Then he exits before I can protest. I am stunned and a little hurt that he is abandoning me so easily, but I do as I have always done and hide my pain under a smile.

I ask, "What are you doing here, Adali? Don't you have two countries to run?"

"As if I could be anywhere else! When we received Warchief Verrick's message, I can't tell you how desperate I felt! You gave us all quite the fright!"

"So everyone tells me. Honestly, it was not on purpose."

"Of course not, Pell. But I am quite angry with you! Taking on the Cabal by yourself with Warchief Verrick, with no backup. You both could have been killed!" Adalind spears me with an icy disapproving look that I know just means that my friend was worried about me.

"At the time it felt like the only choice," I protest, perhaps a touch weakly. "We needed to move before the Cabal realized I was working against them. If we had sent for help, they might have intercepted it."

Adalind keeps the icy look on her face a bit longer before softening. "I know, I know, Pell. Warchief Verrick explained your plan—he was quite adamant in your defense. But it was so dangerous. And to think, they summoned Lord Grazrath. I don't know what we should do about that. With him unleashed on the land, who knows what will happen?"

I shake my head. "And I played right into their hands, bringing Verrick to them, even if delivering him to them was by accident."

"Do not punish yourself too harshly," Adalind says kindly. "It appears they could have used any orc for the ritual. They just wanted Warchief Verrick so that they could make a statement, it seems. If you hadn't cooperated, they would have just kidnapped a different orc and still carried through with the ritual, I'm sure. Who knew that Lord Antony Strand was part of the Cabal! And so unhinged!"

I feel a small twinge of pity for Antony, his soul trapped in the Nether with the archdemons. He was something of a friend to me once. But only a small twinge. Adalind is right that he was unhinged and he apparently hurt and killed many people in pursuit of his ambition. Perhaps his punishment is just, after all.

Adalind continues, "And the others . . . the Council of Thirteen will be quite sparse until we figure this all out."

"The others?"

"Warchief Verrick sent the captain to gather and burn the dead after the incident last week. The captain was able to ascertain the identities of the rest of the Cabal before they were burned. There were members of the Lentley and Wilton duchies, as well as members of the Dadrom and Bellmar countdoms and some smaller noble houses as well. Not the heads of houses, but enough members that it brings up a lot of questions. We may remove those houses from the Council entirely as punishment for their involvement. We cannot risk the Cabal reforming under another banner."

"If the Heads of House weren't involved, I might just levy them with a steep fine or place them on probation. If you act too rashly, you might make enemies where there weren't before."

My friend considers my words and finally nods, "You are, perhaps, right. My own experiences with the Cabal could be clouding my judgment. I want them to be dead and stay dead. Perhaps the probation, along with some public shame, which should hurt their houses' standing for a while. And put more spies in their houses, to be sure that they aren't up to anything."

I nearly choke. "*More* spies?"

She shrugs, "Of course. We cannot risk another war so soon. And Rognar has had spies in Adrik for years. We will just need to expand them in those houses to make sure there aren't any sympathetic to the Cabal left. Especially those who could have a grudge against you or the Warchief for the deaths of their family members."

I take a drink of my water again and find myself very grateful that I am not queen. Regent is bad enough.

Adalind speaks again. "You know, not to go off-topic, but speaking of the Warchief . . ."

I feel my face heat slightly. "What about him?"

"I've heard the most interesting gossip about a certain flirtatious duchess and her pursuit of a taciturn orc . . ."

I smile a little at her teasing. "It is true. Oh, but Adali, I fear I have made such a big mistake!"

My friend instantly goes serious. "Whatever do you mean? Has he hurt you in any way?"

"No! Not at all, but . . ."

So I tell her everything. From the beginning, when I first decided to pursue Verrick to our fake relationship to when it became. And finally, about our fight that we had when he told me that he was falling in love with me.

"You understand, don't you, Adali? Yorian tucked me away in Garden Manor and forced me into his bed. He took total control of my entire life and the whole time he would always go on and on about how he loved me. When Verrick said the same thing and that he wanted to Claim me . . . I . . . I . . ."

"You couldn't help but be reminded of Yorian," Adalind finishes kindly. She has listened intently to my story, though it was long and now the sun outside the window is high in the noonday sky. She shakes her head. "And it wasn't just Yorian with you. Everyone that was supposed to love and protect you just used you instead. Especially your father. It was the same with me, after my real father died and they sent me to House Grimble. The only difference is that I at least had the protection of my brother Marvik . . ." Adalind breaks off, her voice wet with unshed tears. I put my hand out to rest on hers.

"Have they ever found Marvik's body?" I ask gently.

She shakes her head, looking away from me to hide her emotion. "We have sent scouts everywhere, but there's no trace of Marvik nor of Rognar's cousin, Dura, who was fighting him at the Battle of Fort Attis. They fell into the Dense Wood, so we think that wild animals may have gotten ahold of them first . . ." A single tear rolls down Adalind's perfect face, her sorrow over the loss of her brother deep. I can only imagine what it would be like to lose someone that close and then to not even have their body to burn properly. I squeeze down on Adalind's hand, sending as much comfort as I can through the gesture.

"I am truly sorry for your loss, Adali."

My queen brushes away her tears with her other hand, returning my squeeze with the one I still hold. "Thank you, Pell. It is a grief that comes and goes. Someday, perhaps, I will think of Marvik with only joy and not with bitterness. But all that to say, believe me, Pell, I understand exactly what you are saying. I still can barely stand the sound of the orc's *sibilance* because it reminds me of Yorian so much. And when Rognar wanted to Claim me . . ." She gestures to the bite mark she has at the join of her neck and shoulder. For the first time I notice she has dusted it with gold powder, like the kind I use on my eyes, so that the raised ridges glitter in the light, like she is showing off the mark. She continues, "I was terrified. For many reasons. So I understand you, Pell. But Pell . . . "

Adalind looks at me, an expression of the gentle empathy on her flawless features, "You do know . . . you must know, what Yorian gave you, what he forced on you, was not truly love, right?"

I bite my lip hard enough that I feel a sting. "I know that, logically, but my heart . . ."

"Is frightened. I know. Oh, I know Pell." Adalind embraces me again, and again I feel tears come to my eyes. When did I get to be such a weepy woman? I suppose being close to death has knocked loose my emotions. Tightening my eyes, I will the moisture away. I don't want to cry on my royal friend's shoulder.

After a time, Adalind pulls back and looks me square in the eyes, her bearing serious. "I can only tell you what I was told, dear Pell," she says, "and that is that if you don't want to lose him, you must trust him. Trust that he is nothing like Yorian, that his love means something different and is sincere. These orcs are honorable, Pell, and they mean what they say. In fact, after everything the Warchief has gone through, it sounds like it was as hard for him to say the words as it was for you to hear them. You both have deep pain in your pasts that makes you shy towards love. That tells me you can believe his words to be true and that his Claim is not about controlling you, but about being with you always."

I swallow a lump in my throat, thinking about her words. To be with Verrick always . . . that is a dream. It's what I want more than anything. But what if I am wrong and I willingly put myself into a relationship that I can't take back with another male that seeks to control me? If that male were Verrick, it would destroy me.

"How can I dare?" I ask. "How did you dare, with King Rognar?"

My beautiful friend shrugs her shoulders with an effortless grace. "I was told what I am telling you: that if you do not have the courage to give him that trust, you will lose him. Forever."

Adalind reaches out a hand and gives mine a comforting squeeze. "I know it is difficult. The most difficult thing you may ever have to do, opening yourself to such vulnerability. But it can be the best thing too, to have such complete faith in a partner and have them have it in you too . . . and if he ever hurts you, I will have him executed, forthwith."

That surprises a laugh out of me, and I am still laughing when King Rognar enters the room. He gives Adalind a scorching look that makes me feel seriously out of place, before turning a polite gaze on me.

"Regent Santir, I hope you are feeling better? Adalind's been beside herself as you slept."

"I am feeling well, My King, if a tad weak. The healer's work was exceptional."

"Yes," he replies, "I have heard much about the strength of Adrikian healers. I should have them come and teach our Orikesh healers a thing or two. Though the orcish half-elves' innate magic isn't as strong as humans."

"That would be a fine idea," I say back politely, though truth be told, after my interactions with Verrick and Adalind, I am feeling tired and want to rest. The inanities of polite conversation are escaping me.

"Well," declares the king, "I do not mean to interrupt the conversation of friends, but it is past time for luncheon and I have come to retrieve my queen."

"You could have sent a servant to do that," smiles Adalind.

"Then I would not have the pleasure of escorting my wife across the castle," teases back Rognar.

They are too adorable, just as I remember them to be when I saw them last at Garden Manor. I am truly happy for my friend that she has her happy ending. Could I truly have the same if I listen to her words? If I can give Verrick my trust? I am beginning to think I want to try.

"King Rognar?" I ask. The two rulers leave their teasing to look at me. "After the luncheon repast, could you send Warchief Verrick to my room? I have something that I need to discuss with him."

Adalind smiles at my words, but Rognar frowns. "I am sorry Regent Santir, I thought you knew. Warchief Verrick and his orcs left nearly an hour ago to head back to High Citadel. It was not long after you woke up."

"He did what?" Adalind and I ask at the same time. We exchange a look, Adalind's wide-eyed with confusion and me with incredulous rage. For I am angry. He wants to avoid me so badly that he will leave me so soon? Oh, that will not do at all.

I try to stand up, saying, "Where is my horse? I need to go catch him."

But Adalind shoos me back into bed, a stern look on her face, "Oh no, you don't. You still need your rest. Healers' orders. You just barely woke from a sleep that lasted a week. You cannot seriously think of riding all the way back to High Citadel. Even an hour's ride is too much for you right now. Not to mention you'd be on horseback and they are on warbeasts, so you'd have to set a punishing pace to catch them. No, your talk with the Warchief will have to wait until you are entirely better."

Defeated, I lay back on my pillows. But my heart burns with indignation toward Verrick. He wants to avoid me, does he? Well, as soon as the healer allows me, I will follow him. I aim to talk to him soon.

He can't avoid me forever.

CHAPTER 27

Verrick

A week passes until the day the news that I have both expected and dreaded reaches me in the human capital.

"Regent Santir is back," Friza reports, coming to the room in the palace I use as an office. "She has just arrived at the gates."

My heart lurches in my chest and my Mating Instinct beats furiously at its confines, desperate to see her. Has she regained all her strength? Is she well? Is she as lost without me as I am without her? But I pull back using my iron control. I swore that if she escaped the Nether and returned to the land of the living that I would never bother her with my feelings again. That I would ask nothing of her that she does not willingly give.

So I merely grunt at Friza and say, "It is good that she is back. The Council has missed her guidance."

It is a neutral, diplomatic thing to say. Almost human in its way of saying something and nothing all at once. I hate it. But if I let my longing show, I know Friza will push me to go see Pellia, to speak to her, to beg her to choose me, to accept my love. But I will not do that. I won't bother her with something she found so distressing before, especially when she is so newly healed.

Friza rolls her eyes at my non-answer, as if entirely tired of my nonsense. "Why can you not go to her? I still don't entirely understand why we left."

"I made a vow." I speak the words solemnly, even as I wonder after Pellia. Is she in the castle or still in the courtyard? Where will she go first? Perhaps I can watch her from afar and assuage the tearing feelings of my Mating Instinct, to at least assure myself that she is well and taken care of.

My second merely laughs bitterly at me. "Ah, yes. The vow to 'never ask anything' of the regent again if she woke up. But what if she wants you to ask something of her? I told you, you didn't see how desperate she was when you were missing. Even as I suspected her, I could see that she was distressed. Now that I know she was innocent . . ."

"She is a kind person. Of course, she would be distressed if she thought someone was in peril."

"It was more than kindness!" exclaims Friza. "She has feelings for you! Any fool can see that—just as any fool can see that you have feelings for her. Why make this complicated?"

"You do not know the full story."

"Then tell it to me. I want to know why you are miserable and why you insist on staying like that!"

I hesitate slightly, but finally say, "Before I was taken . . . Pellia and I . . . we fought."

Friza nods. "Yes, she told me, though she only told me it was about Claiming. Why fight about that?"

That makes me hesitate again. Am I telling things that Pellia would rather were not shared? But I need to make Friza understand, so she stops pushing. So I continue, "We fought because I told her I loved her, that . . . I wanted to Claim her. She has things in her past that made it so that she did not react well to those words. She accused me of wanting to own her."

"And you explained that's not what Claiming means for orcs?"

"I tried . . . but she left before I could." I finish lamely.

"Then all the more reason you should talk to her! This is all a misunderstanding. You would deprive yourself of the one you love over a misunderstanding? That does not sound like the Warchief I know."

I shake my head. "You don't understand. You weren't there. The idea of me loving her . . . it made her panic. I will not risk upsetting her again, not when she is recovering."

"She is done recovering," insists my second, "or the healer would not have let her travel. You owe it to both of you to figure this out, not run from it!"

"You don't understand," I repeat, "and I am done having this conversation. You are dismissed, Friza."

My second looks at me with fire in her eyes, indignation warring with duty, but I know that her pride will only allow duty to win in the end. So she nods at me, noticeably not doing the fists of respect on her chest, and leaves the room.

It only takes me a few minutes to realize that I've made a mistake. With Friza there to distract me, I at least wasn't pining for Pellia, but with no one there to divert my thoughts, they settle on my beloved human and will not move away from them. For the next hour, I am tormented by my thoughts of her and of Friza's admonishment. Could it be so easy as just talking? Could I have Pellia back in my life? But I am bound by my oath and I will not break it. I am an orc of honor and honor is all I have left, now that Pellia is lost to me.

I get no work done as I sit in my office stewing. When there is a sharp rap on the door, I am most eager to have someone, anyone, to break me out of my melancholy yearning.

"Enter."

Friza enters again, looking annoyed. "The Council is at it again. They demand that a regent come and settle their arguments."

Was there a Council meeting that I forgot about? It is possible. My mind has been all over the place lately. Standing from my chair, I say, "I will go. You did not let them bother Pellia, did you?"

Friza shakes her head. "No, I knew you wouldn't want that. I told them I'd fetch you."

As much as I disdain being something for my second to come "fetch" for the convenience of a bunch of humans, I am glad she did so. Pellia doesn't need to put up with their nonsense so soon after returning. She should be gathering her strength, not have it sapped by whining insects, buzzing about with political agendas.

I follow Friza through the castle, but again, I am distracted. Everywhere we go, my body is tuned to Pellia. My eyes search for her presence. *Just to make sure she is alright*, I tell myself. *She looked so small a week ago in her bed.* But I don't get a glimpse, which only makes the Mating Instinct in me more frantic.

I'm so focused on trying to find Pellia, I do not even notice that we have arrived at the Council Chamber and it takes me a moment to realize . . . I do not hear any voices coming from within. I look at my second, confused, and still step in. Only to find that the Council is not there, but Pellia is, standing on the other side of the room, across the Council Chamber.

I whirl toward my second-in-command and she merely shrugs. "Sorry, My Warchief," Friza says, backing out of the room. "But I owed her a favor and this is how she aimed to claim it."

Then my second is gone, the door shut behind her. I hear the lock turn and click, and then I am alone in the Council Chamber with Pellia.

She steps forward and I can feel my heart lighten, even as fear fills me as well. It is good to see her standing, looking hale and hearty, even as recrimination shines in her beautiful eyes. We are both silent for a few moments, as she moves forward, around the table and closer to me. The seconds tick away as we stare at each other. I long to rush toward her, to take her in my arms, to take her lips with mine. To let her know over and over that I belong to her, and that I hope against hope that she belongs to me as well.

Finally, when she is a few feet away, she speaks, breaking our charged silence. "You left me."

Her words are like blows. They are succinct and accusatory, shooting straight to my heart. I respond, "I had to."

"Why? Why did you have to?"

My feelings are on the tip of my tongue, but I swallow them down. I shake my head. "I cannot tell you that. Please do not ask me." If she asks me, I will tell her again how I love her, how I long for her, and I swore I would not burden her with those declarations again.

We are silent again. I can see the hurt in her eyes, in the carriage of her body. I am confused. How could I be hurting her when all I am seeking to do is what she wants?

She breaks the silence again. "Very well. I won't ask you again. But I won't let you run from me any longer, Verrick," Pellia speaks passionately, her voice raising slightly with her agitation. "I have something that I need to say to you."

"Then say it," I reply. The sooner she says what she needs to say, the sooner I can leave. Being here with her is like that sweetest kind of torture. And while I may not break under pain, I am certain that if I spend too much time in her presence, it will not be long before I break my vow to her. She makes me feel weak against her.

She shocks me with what she says. "I am falling in love with you, Verrick ka Rocknir."

What? My ears must be deceiving me. When I say nothing back, out of surprise, she continues, "That is what you said to me those many days past, is it not? Well, now it is true for me as it was for you. Or rather, I *am* in love with you. I have had a full week to think on it and I am sure now. Well, as sure as I can be. I still have my old fears and doubts but, I will face them to tell you that I love you, too."

She suddenly looks wary. "Or at least I hope it is 'too.' Unless . . . you've changed your mind?"

Changed my mind? *Changed my mind*? I can barely keep myself from rushing to the woman and prostrating myself on bended knee, I am so happy. But my wariness holds me back. "But before, you said . . ."

"I know what I said," interrupts Pellia. "I was confused. Frightened! The only other person who had ever told me that he loved me before was Yorian. And when you said you wanted to

Claim me . . . when you said it . . . it opened old wounds. But I am trying to move past them, to not let Yorian control my future as he did my past. But I must know . . . do you still want me, or am I too late?"

In a moment, I traverse the few feet between us, and Pellia is in my arms. *Where she belongs.* My Mating Instinct purrs in approval. She melts in my embrace and I say, "I want you Pellia. I want everything about you. And if you need a champion, give me these demons that plague you, that I may slay them."

Pellia laughs lightly and looks up from the protection of my arms and teases, "Does this mean that you'll kiss me now? Or will you make me beg? I know how you like that."

I groan slightly and fall in her, my lips finding hers in a bruising kiss. I pour all my hope and joy into her, as well as my relief and a little of the fear that I have been living with. She responds in kind, meeting me with nip for nip and stroke for stroke, her passion as bruising as my own. And I welcome it, all of it, wanting her to leave her mark on my body. I even welcome her little bites that she gives me, as the pinpricks of pain remind me that this is real and that I am not dreaming. Pellia is here. She loves me. She is willing to fight her demons for me. I am the most fortunate orc.

"You are well?' I ask between deep kisses. "You have your strength?"

"Very well," she responds, as some teasing nips with her lips. "Strong enough to take you in whatever way you want me."

I groan at her seductive words. The kiss deepens still and soon I am lifting my little mate up in my arms and carry her toward the massive Council Table. I perch her on the edge and growl, "I have wanted to fuck you on this table since the first moment that I saw you sitting across it a month ago."

"Oh, you beast, you absolutely shouldn't." Pellia playfully taps my shoulder, letting me know that she absolutely thinks I *should.*

"Why not?" I tease back, lowering my head to skim her throat with my nose, breathing in the heady aroma of Pellia and her natural musk, before kissing my way lightly up her sensitive skin before claiming her lips again. "Does that thought make you too wet, Regent Santir?"

Pellia laughs, a delighted sound, and reaches for my belt, saying, "Why don't you find out, Warchief Verrick?"

With another growl, I push Pellia back onto the table, and she laughs again at my eagerness. Her legs splay wide and my hands travel up under her skirts, finding the evidence of her arousal. Without hesitation, I sink to my knees and flip up her skirts, questing my way to her center. With my first lick, she jolts and moans, encouraging my efforts. I hitch my arms around her thighs and pull her to meet my mouth more fully. Then I fuck her with my mouth in earnest. Every cry and sigh she makes just leads me to redouble my efforts. I shove my long orc tongue into her willing pussy and she cries, reaching her climax faster than she ever has before. It is like her body is primed for me, ready to meet my every pleasure. I begin to thrum, pushing her climax higher, until it crests again and she orgasms a second time, her channel milking my tongue. I move back to licking her swollen clit with soft, slow movements, letting her settle down from the peak of her pleasure before speeding up again, this time taking one of my hands and adding my fingers into her cunt. I pump in relentlessly, teasing, licking, nipping, and sucking at her clit, when with a sob she comes again.

Finally, she cries out, "No more foreplay! I want you, Verrick."

"What is it you want?" I tease, perhaps a little cruel in the face of her desperation.

"Your cock!" she replies instantly, knowing my game. She scoots her delicious-looking pussy closer to the edge of the table and says, "Please Verrick, give me your cock. I need it, please!"

"You're right," I say, while undoing my belt and letting my warkilt fall to the floor, "I do like your begging."

With that, I seat myself fully in my beautiful beloved and she lets out a pleasured shriek as she comes again. I piston and roll my hips, thrumming all the while, lengthening her orgasm until tears are rolling down her lovely cheeks. When her orgasm is done, I thrum harder, priming her body to take me again and start pumping my hips.

She chokes and says, "Gods save me. I'd almost forgotten that your cock vibrates!"

"Then I will remind you so thoroughly that you will never forget, my mate."

We both freeze the moment the words are out of my lips, but I will not take them back. She tenses for a moment and then, after what is probably only a few seconds but feels like eternity, she relaxes. "That's what I am, isn't it? I'm your mate now."

"You were always my mate," I respond, rolling my hips again in a circle and making her gasp. "We were just too stubborn to realize it for a while."

"No longer," she says, meeting my thrust and increasing the pleasure for both of us. "I'm yours and you are mine. My mate."

The pleasure I feel at her taking ownership of me almost makes my eyes cross. "Yes, your mate. Yours."

I pump my hips harder and faster, chasing my own climax. Pleasure shoots up my spine as I feel it take me. "I love you, Pellia! I love you!"

She orgasms with me, squeezing down hard on my cock, taking my wits with her as she climaxes. She gasps and moans and I collapse, falling on my forearms, careful not to crush the dainty human with my muscular bulk.

She kisses my forehead, so gently as she comes down, then covers my face in soft, fluttering kisses before she says, "I love you too, My Warchief. My mate. My Verrick."

EPILOGUE

Pellia

The torches burn bright in the darkness and the rhythm of the drums beat in time with percussion of my heart. I can barely believe where I am: my Mating Ceremony. My own Bride Chase, like the one I attended months ago for Queen Adalind. But now the one that is standing in front of a crowd of orcs and humans in a scandalously revealing tunic and leggings is me.

My dear friend Adalind works with Friza to trace runes on the bare parts of my skin with a paste of berries. *Soro* berries. I am told that they are thought to be aphrodisiacs in Orikesh culture, but I don't think I need them. As the orcs chant and drum and Verrick stares at me with dark, lustful eyes, I am already filled with a squirming feeling of arousal. A frenetic energy fills my limbs, anticipation wanting to push me forward. I am ready to be chased. *And fucked*, I add silently to myself.

They draw the last rune on my cheek, and, abruptly, the drums stop. Verrick steps forward, all brooding and simmering with barely leashed passion, ready for us to exchange the traditional words, and I smile at him. I never thought I would want to be here, binding myself to only one male, but when that male is Verrick . . . well, there's no place else I'd rather be.

I stumble a little over the Orikesh words, the language more guttural than my voice wants to be. I just hope they aren't intelligible, as I say, *"Pah threy thik. Thik drad vik or brok. Thik drad jro hana. Thik drad Kor Verrick tay."*

I will run. Run until the world falls away. Run until ti
Run until you catch me, Warchief Verrick.

Verrick growls, an eager sound, as if hearing me speak his language pleases him. Hmm. If that is enough to arouse him, then maybe I will have to put more effort into learning his language. Or at least the important words like, "Fuck me," and "Now."

My nerves ratchet up as he responds to me with the traditional reply. I know it basically means that he swears to chase me and catch me, that there's nowhere I can run that will hide from him. Something to that effect. But after his words, I am going to add my own spin to the ceremony that I know will surprise my mate, and the thought makes me nervous.

My mate. It's still strange to think of Verrick like that and though he has not given me the Claiming Bite yet, in our hearts, it is true. He is mine and I am his. I still feel panicked about that sometimes, but rather than run from him, I speak with him and talk through my fears. Verrick is always there as a patient, stalwart influence, always willing to listen and that helps. The fears are coming up less and less lately and I know it is because he and I are meant to be.

The drums begin again, and I realize Verrick has stopped talking. It's time for me to run. But before turning to run up the mountain, I catch Verrick's smoldering gaze with my own. Very deliberately, I raise up my hand and take off my ring, the one with the contraception charm on it. His eyes widen at the action. We've been talking lately about having children, but this is blatant action, an invitation for him to *breed* me. I drop the ring on the ground as his eyes dilate, nostrils flaring as I laugh, before turning and running into the woods.

I am not a warrior with their muscles and training, but I give it my best effort. Running as fast as I am able, I weave in and out of the trees with abandon. I have no destination in mind, just that I need to put as much distance between us as possible. I know, logically, that Verrick will make up the distance in no time at all, that my efforts are very much in vain. But I don't listen to that part of my mind; no, I tap into a deeper, more primal part of me that makes me into willing prey and run.

My lungs are burning with exertion when I hear a roar behind me and know that the chase has started. They must have finished preparing Verrick with his own runes. The sound makes my heart pound both with anticipation and maybe a little fear. Just enough to push my limbs to move with renewed energy. I laugh again, ready to play with my mate.

Soon I find myself deep in the woods, the trees getting thicker and more wild with every step. I am pushing through the undergrowth when I hear a familiar growl echo behind me. With a gasp, I turn and see Verrick stalking slowly toward me. I turn and push harder, trying to get away, but I hear him pounce behind me and soon I am thrown over his shoulder, being carried off to wherever he wants me.

"Let me go, you awful brute!" I tease, helplessly hitting his well-muscled back with my tiny human fists.

His only response is to thrum. Instantly I feel myself getting wet, priming myself for what my body really wants. I choke out a laugh and say, "That is not fair!"

"What is not fair," growls Verrick as he puts me carefully on a patch of soft moss on the ground, "is that my mate apparently wants me to get her with kit and didn't warn me. *That* is not fair."

With his words, he tears the leather leggings away from my body, shredding them in his haste, and I gasp as the cool night air hits my wet center. His thrumming intensifies as he stares down at me, his eyes completely black as his eyes are dilated with arousal.

"Tell me, my mate, my love," he says, his voice thick with his sibilance, "is that what you really want? For me to fill you with my seed again and again until you carry our child?"

I moan at the thought, surprising myself. I knew I was ready to be with Verrick in that way, and I even knew that it would make his Mating Instincts wild, but I didn't know that it would arouse me so much. Splaying my thighs open in a blatant invitation, I wait, but Verrick doesn't move.

"Say it," he says, "I want to hear it."

"Yes," I gasp out, moving my hands down my body to brush the apex of my entrance, teasing my mate with my actions as I delicately trace my clit, "I want your seed, Verrick. I want your child. I want everything."

He growls, grabbing my fingers and putting them in his mouth to suck my juices off of them, thrumming harder as he does so. A light orgasm takes me, just from the strength of his *sibilance,* and I whimper in ecstasy. Within moments his warkilt is gone and I feel him notch his maleness at my pussy.

"Remember, you asked for this," he warns. "I'll never let you go now, my mate."

Before I can say that I don't want him to let me go, ever, he invades my body, conquering my pleasure with every push of his hips. His cock vibrates inside me, stimulating me in ways that only he can, and I am screaming with every thrust. My second climax takes me by surprise, so soon after my first and I am flying and falling to pieces, pleasure skittering along the surface of my skin and firing through every muscle. I clench around him, milking his cock with all my strength and he growls before taking me and flipping me onto my belly, my ass in the air as he tilts my hips so that he can go deeper, knocking on my womb. Every touch makes my eyes roll into the back of my head, shouting my pleasure. They can probably hear me all the way in High Citadel, but I don't care. I abandon myself to the pleasure of his possessive, powerful mastery of me.

"Take me, woman," he commands. "Take all of me!"

"Yes, Verrick, yes!" I cry out as the speed of his pistoning hips increases, losing all rhythm as he pounds into me with abandon. Then he freezes behind me, all his muscles locking as he comes, his seed pouring into me and presses deep, extending my pleasure with his own. He is coming more than usual and I can feel his spend leaking out of me, sliding down my thighs. Verrick collapses on my back, warming me as his bulk shields me from the cool air and he kisses up my spine all the way to my neck. Each caress of his lips causes little sparks of delight to dance over my skin and I stretch into him, searching for more affection. His lips find the join of my neck and shoulder, and his kisses turn into little nips from his fangs and tusks. I can almost read his mind, knowing what he is thinking, even as he holds himself back.

"Do it," I say impulsively, moving my head to ease his access.

Verrick stills behind me. I feel his shock, even as his arms move around me to hold me closer, his breath on my skin.

"Do you mean it? Pellia . . . if I Claim you . . ."

"I want it," I state it with utter surety. "I want you. Forever, Verrick. No more running, no more doubt. I want us to belong to each other."

He thrums again, my tired body filling with energy and arousal as he does so. I stir underneath him and flip over so that we are front to front. Taking his lips with mine, I feel his *sibilance* grow stronger, my pleasure once again heading toward its peak.

"It might hurt," Verrick warns, his expression serious, even as his eyes are dark with hunger and possession, "I will time it right so that it happens when you have your most pleasure to balance it out."

"I trust you," I return, stretching again and luxuriating in the feel of our naked flesh stroking together. I tease my fingers down his well-built chest and over his stomach, finding his cock with my fingers and pump his harness brutally in my grip, the way I know drives him wild. "But do not make me wait too long, my mate, or I may start running again."

A savage light takes over his eyes at the thought and an animalistic growl mixes with his thrumming, making me smile. Perhaps I should try to run again, after all. I squirm under his weight as if to leave, but he bears down on me, pressing my back into the soft moss and he grinds into me, stimulating my clit with his cock. I whimper again as another light orgasm takes me, priming my body to be ready for him once more.

"Later," he says, still moving his hips and building yet another small orgasm, "Later I will run and chase you _____. Many times our whole lives, I will chase you, little temptress, but for now I have you right where I want you."

With a slight tilt of his hips, he notches into my entrance and slowly plunders into my depths. I move to try and match his thrust, to increase the pace and pressure, but he is holding me down and I am helpless but to take what he gives me. I groan as he fully seats himself inside me, but then the damn orc doesn't move. I push again with my hips, but still I am held still but his bulk on my body.

"Move!" I command, feeling the building frenzy inside of me.

His only response is to thrum harder and I feel myself build up to my peak before he stops. I laugh and whine in equal measure as I realize his game.

"Not this again!" I complain, snaking my hands down to my clit, wanting to give myself some relief, but he takes my naughty, questing hands in one of his own and holds my hands up above my head.

"No, no, no," he chides, a cruel smile playing at his lips. "You said you trusted me. Now show me. Surrender to me, temptress."

I go to protest again, but his thrum starts and I just moan, feeling my inner muscles squeeze down on his hard malehood, pleasure building in blinding waves and then he stops. I choke off an indignant whine. But then he goes again and again. Occasionally, he pushes with his hips, rolling a shallow rhythm inside me that only teases me further. When I am a tangled ball of nerve endings, all alight with almost too much pleasure, his lips finally find the join between my neck and shoulder again.

"Mine," he thrums, his voice almost completely taken over by *sibilance*. With that word, he finally, *finally*, draws out and slams home with his cock. That one thrust sends everything over the edge, the largest and longest orgasm of my life over-taking me just as his teeth sink into my flesh. Pain mingles with pleasure, sending me to heights I didn't even know that my body was capable of. I am exploding and mending, everything lighting up, even as I am grounded beneath my love.

A moment, or maybe eternity, passes. Verrick nurses the wound at my neck as I wind down. And there, underneath all the pleasure and the raw feeling, I feel a second emotion. Like a second heartbeat, right next to my own. I feel love and awe and, yes, possessive reverence. Verrick's emotions, now at home in my chest and I know that mine are in his. We are tangled up in each other, two halves to a whole, mates now in the truest sense of the word.

As I turn in his arms and feel his love for me feed my love for him, I take his lips again, tasting a little of my blood, and know that I am exactly where I am meant to be: loved by the orc Warchief.

The End.

**Turn the page to read a special Sneak Preview of the
Third Book in
The War Brides of Adrik:**

War Maiden

BONUS CHAPTER

Marvik

Pain is the first thing that I feel as consciousness crowds my senses. A deep, aching pain in my chest, almost as if I was stabbed with a sword. A quick flash of memory comes to me. Of a knife flashing in the sun, flicking under my parry and finding its home in my chest. Of bright green eyes looking into mine with a mix of shock and horror and maybe a little hate. Of my falling to the ground, sliding away into darkness, welcoming the embrace of the Nether as I entered death, unafraid.

But this is too much pain to be dead. I open my eyes and find myself looking at the rocky ceiling of a cave, stalactites pointing down at me threateningly, like swords of stone dangling above my head. The light is dim and orange, lit by a torch or firepit just out of my range of vision.

Nothing makes sense. Where am I? How am I not dead? I try to sit up, but pain shoots through me and steals my strength. I groan involuntarily, my vision whiting out and I begin to fall back, when strong arms catch me and slowly lower back into my bedding.

"Easy now," an alluring and smoky voice says. "It's not time for you to wake yet. You still have much healing to do."

A healer then? Did I somehow survive the orcress' blow? Am I still at Fort Attis? No, that can't be. There are no caves in Fort Attis. My vision is still gone as the healer lays me back. I feel healing magic flow into my chest, soothing the pain and allowing my whited-out and blurred vision to return.

With my eyes open, I seek my savior and am shocked. Before me is an orcress. Not any orcress, but the one from my memories. The one who stabbed me!

"You!" I gasp out and try to jerk back. But my muscles are weak from disuse and she easily holds me down, keeping me in place.

"Me," she agrees, grimacing lightly. "Stay still or you will open your wound again."

My first reaction is to disobey. I am obviously the prisoner of the orcs and the first duty of a captured soldier is to resist and escape. But her words also make a lot of sense. I can't escape if I'm dead.

So I warily let myself sink into the bedroll. It's a rough rest place, just a blanket over a pile of leaves. I can hear the crinkle of the dead foliage crushing as I lay back. What kind of holding is this for prisoners? I can't see the entrance to the cave from my vantage point, nor any other captured soldiers. I am unbound, with no ropes or chains to hold me in position. Perhaps they figure I am not a flight risk, injured as I am. But why save me in the first place? I know the orcress struck a death blow. I could feel it when her knife sunk in. Why are they wasting resources to keep me alive? It makes no sense.

"Where am I?" I ask, not really expecting an answer. Captors have no reason to answer a captive's questions, after all.

The orcress surprises me by placing a hand on my chest. More healing magic enters me, soothing the ache of my wound and lulls me to relax further. She says, "We are in a cave. I believe your people would say that it's in the Deep Wood."

The Deep Wood? The one that surrounds Fort Attis? Why are the orcs holding here? If the fort has fallen, they should push their advantage and head north. Unless they already have and have just left the prisoners behind.

The orcress' hand leaves my chest and I feel better than I have since I awoke. I am tempted to try to sit up again, but think better of it. Something tells me that the healing won't last if I move too much.

"How long have I been asleep?" I ask, pressing my luck since the orcress seems to be in an answering mood.

"About a month."

"A *month*?" I repeat incredulously. Perhaps that is why there are no other prisoners. They must have already been moved to Orikesh work camps. The country has, no doubt, fallen to the orcish onslaught. And my sister . . .

"What have you done to the queen?" I demand, "What have you done with Adalind?"

The orcress goes still and then looks at me deliberately. There's something hard in her eyes and something very like suspicion. "Why do you care?" she finally asks. "Is she your lover?"

I sputter, feeling a little sick at the question. "She's my sister! Please, just tell me what they have done with her."

That seems to bring the orcress up short and when she looks at me again, there's pity mixed into her gaze. "I don't know," she responds. "But I do know that last I heard they were not planning on letting her live."

Pain slices through me again, this time in my heart. Adalind, dead? But wait, why is the orcress speaking as if she doesn't know? She was with their king when they broke through our defenses, side by side with their top generals. She must be very high-ranking, so why doesn't she know what has happened to Adalind?

"Who are you?" I ask, not caring that I sound belligerent. If they have indeed hurt my sister, then we are still enemies, no matter if she is healing me or not.

"I am Dura," she responds, though she doesn't expound on her clan or rank.

The name seems familiar, almost as if I have heard it before. Heard her tell it to me in some distant past.

"Have you told me this?" I ask.

"Many times," she returns, turning away from me and moving toward the glow of the fire. "You never remember in the heat of your fevers."

I do not feel fevered now, my mind clear, even as I am confused. Every piece of information she so willingly hands me only brings up more questions.

"Where are my men? Where are the other prisoners?"

"I don't know where your men are, though when I left the fort it did not appear that there were going to be many prisoners."

"When *you* left? You are no longer with the orcs?"

The orcress visibly flinches at my question, as if my words are painful to her. She turns around again, bringing a cup of steaming liquid toward me. "No," she answers curtly before tilting my head up and bringing the cup to my lips. "I am not with the other orcs anymore."

I take a sip of what she's offering me, not that I am left with much choice not to. It's a broth of some sort, bitter and herbaceous without enough salt. But I feel the warmth seep into my weakened limbs and nutrients fill my bloodstream. I eagerly take another sip and another until the cup is empty.

Filled with broth, I can think even more clearly. It is becoming obvious that we are not with the other orcs. We are alone, this strange orcress and I. But why are we separated from the others? Why am I not a prisoner or dead? Did the orcress desert the Horde and if so, why?

Pulling away from the cup, I stare directly into the orcress' eyes. They are a bright green, and glint like gemstones upon her face, which is more delicate than other orcs I have seen. One of her parents must have been an elf or nymph. "Why am I here?" I demand, holding her eyes with mine. "What do you want with me?"

"You are here because I brought you here. I took you from the thick of battle and saved you with my magic. As to what I want . . ." She pauses, then grimaces. After what seems like forever, she finally continues, "It appears you are my *Ash'ka*."

The word is unfamiliar to me. "*Ash'ka*? What is that?"

She bites the top of her lip, a hint of fang showing as she

does. The warm light illuminates her deep green skin and high cheekbones. She stands still as a statue, assessing me with her emerald gaze before finally answering me.

"It's elvish. It means you are my mate. My soulmate."

What? *What?*

AFTERWARD

It's done! You finished! Hooray! Thank you so much for reading my second book in the War Brides of Adrik *series. This one fought me a little bit. I've read other romance writers who talk about how sometimes characters don't want to go together easily, that they have to fight to get the characters together, and I very much experienced that with this book. From the very beginning, I knew that Pellia and Verrick belonged together, but the more I wrote, the less they wanted to be together. Their trauma was too conflicting, I guess. Nevertheless, I soldiered on, believing in the premise of my book. I won't lie, a couple times I really thought I'd have to trash the whole thing and start over, but eventually, with a little help from Friza, they got together and I'm super happy with how it all came out. Hopefully, you are too.*

As usual, I'd like to thank my editor, Baylee Mehl. You catch things I can't and I know that this whole book is better because of your work and friendship.

In that same vein, I'd like to thank my beta readers, Valerie Joseph and S. A. Huff. I so appreciate you guys taking time out of your busy lives and schedules to help me. I am really thankful for all that you do.

I would also like to thank Anne-Marie (monsterromancereader) for sending me some typos that she found. You totally rock!

Next up are Marvik and Dura! Yes, Marvik is alive. Those of you who caught my foreshadowing in the first two books were right. The next book is going to take us back to the Battle of Fort Attis, in the thick of battle. Dura and Marvik fight and then Dura has to make a decision. I don't want to spoil too much for you going forward, but I will say that I am excited about the twists and turns of their adventure as they come together. Look for the next book to be coming out in just a few months.

Lastly, whether or not you liked the book, please consider leaving a review on Amazon. The feedback will help me grow as a writer and know if you guys want to see more War Brides *or not. Again, if you found an error while reading, please email authorjordynalexander@gmail.com so that we can remedy it for a future edition.*

Thanks!

Jordyn Alexander

Want More?
Sign up for my Newsletter at jordynalexander.net for an exclusive bonus epilogue for both War Queen *and* War Mistress!
(Don't worry about me flooding your inbox.
Newsletters go out only once a quarter)

GLOSSARY

Characters

Humans

Pellia ka Roknir, née Santir: The female main character of *War Mistress*. The daughter of a duke. Pellia was forced to be the mistress of King Yorian when she turned twenty and was his mistress until he died, some twelve years later. She was appointed the Regent of Adrik. She is mated to Verrick ka Roknir, the orcish Regent of Adrik.

Adalind ka Woreki, née Cutter: The female main character of *War Queen*. She was originally born the peasant daughter of a woodcutter before two fairies blessed her with beauty and the love of a great king, which led her to be forcibly married to the evil king Yorian. She outlived him and is married and mated to Rognar, King of the Orcs. This makes her the queen of both Adrik and Orik.

Ursa Malloy: The daughter of a lesser noble house, Ursa is the Head Lady-in-Waiting to Adalind. She's quiet and not much is known about her personal life, but she was engaged to one of King Yorian's personal guard who died in the war. She is now in charge of Garden Manor and the Bride Pool the orcs can pick mates from.

Dame Zera Orden: The only daughter of Count Orden and the only female knight in Adrik. Her appointment was only approved because King Yorian wanted to make sure that

Adalind's closest knight couldn't have a bastard with her, which he was always paranoid about. Zera is extremely skilled, but has a lot of doubts and insecurities. She was assigned to find the remaining Cabal members with Urim.

Sir Marvik Grimble: The only son of House Grimble and the adopted brother of Queen Adalind. Presumed dead. He was the only one to be kind to Adalind, as she was growing up as a ward of House Grimble and is extremely dutiful and honorable, something that separated him from his parents and gave them a strained relationship. He rose through the ranks to become Captain of the Blue Guard, the king's personal guard. He was last seen at the Battle of Fort Attis fighting King Rognar's cousin, Dura ka Woreki.

Orcs

Verrick ka Roknir: The male main character of *War Mistress*. The leader of the largest clan in Orik and also leader of the largest contingent of the Horde. His father was an orc and his mother was a siren. He has gray-green skin, tusks, tattoos on his face and chest, and is almost seven feet tall. His sibilance is very strong, and he can use a siren's death scream under dire circumstances. He is mated to Pellia.

Rognar ka Woreki: The male main character of *War Queen*. The king of the orc kingdom of Orik. His father was an orc and his mother is a troll. He has pine green skin, double tusks, ram's horns, and is almost seven feet tall. He is very skilled in battle and rules well. His voice was ruined as a baby, so he has no sibilance.

Gunag ka Strock: The right hand of the king. His father was an orc and his mother was an elf. He has lighter green skin, pointed ears, fangs as opposed to tusks, and is about six and a half feet tall. Considered pretty for an orc, Gunag is very insecure about being considered weaker than other orcs and this makes him hot-headed. He is very interested in Dame Zera, who does not return his interest.

Urim ka Churnok: The left hand of the king. His father was a human and his mother was an orc. He has dark green skin, tusks, a scar on his cheek, and is a little over six and a half feet tall. He is quiet and crafty and the leader of Orik's spies. He is currently working with Dame Zera to uncover the rest of the Cabal.

Friza ka Roknir: Verrick's second-in-command. Her mother was an orcress and her father was a troll. She has forest-green skin with double tusks and two small horns and is around six feet tall. She is extremely accomplished as a warrior, having worked her way up to being second in the Roknir clan with not only her skills on the battlefield but with her reputation for loyalty and forthrightness.

Korovi ka Roknir: The most skilled fighter in the Roknir clan. His mother was an orcress and his father was human. He has lighter green skin with one set of tusks and fangs and is a little over six feet tall. He has no interest in leading and has never challenged for warchief, a fact that Verrick acknowledges that if Korovi did, it isn't clear who would win. His valor in defending Pellia sees him granted leave to go to Garden Manor to find a bride at the end of *War Mistress*.

Larek ka Lowek: A member of the Horde who Pledged himself to Adalind's service. His father is a troll and his mother is an orc and they are still together. He has pine green skin, double tusks, ram's horns, and is seven feet tall. He is a little naïve and dreams of glory. Turnog is his identical twin.

Turnog Ka Lowek: A member of the Horde that Pledged himself to Adalind's service. His father is a troll and his mother is an orc and they are still together. He has pine green skin, double tusks, ram's horns, and is seven feet tall. He is an outstanding warrior but prefers books to fighting. Larek is his identical twin.

Dura Ka Woreki: An orcress shieldmaiden and Rognar's cousin. Presumed dead. Her father is an orc and her mother is an elf. She has lighter green skin, fangs, and pointed ears and is six feet tall. She was last seen fighting Adalind's foster brother, Lord Marvik at the Battle of Fort Attis.

Misc

Melelea Shadowsdottir: Rognar's mother and Adalind's friend, confidant, and lady-in-waiting. She is a troll and has gray skin, dark purple hair, small horns, and double tusks. She was mated to Rognar's father, who was abusive, and escaped his plot to murder her when she was of no use to him. She is adept at illusion magic and reads tarot cards along with the stars to see the future.

Orikesh Words and Terms

The King's Axe: The king's right hand, leader of his armies, and his personal bodyguard and occasional executioner. The advisor that carries out all open, above-board actions of the king.

The King's Shield: The king's left hand, leader of his spies, information network, and occasionally his assassin. The advisor that carries out all the shadowy dark deeds commanded by the king.

Sibilance: An orc's ability to spur arousal with their voices. It involves thrumming (a purring hum) that causes arousal and increases climatic pleasure when used during sex. It also causes orc voices to be very smooth and pleasing to the ear.

Ka: Means "of Clan" i.e. Rognar ka Woreki is Rognar of Clan Woreki.

Garoth ya. Larok ta. Perthik o kari. Garoth ya: The traditional chant done during the Bride Chase to increase the libido and arousal of those involved. Roughly translated, it means: *Come to me. I wait for you. We shall be as one. Come to me.*

Lir: Queen

Lor: King

Kor: Warchief

Stratkthri: A type of undead that spreads curses through its bite. Very dangerous. Can be killed by removing its head and burning it so that it can't come back.

Adrikian High Noble Houses (Members With Council Seats)

Howser: A dead house. A duchy. This was the lineage of Yorian, and he died without leaving an heir, causing the name to become extinct.

Grimble: A dead house. A duchy. With the deaths of Duke Grimble and his son, as well as the arresting and stripping of titles done to Duchess Grimble, this name and house are now extinct.

Kimber: A duchy.

Lentley: A duchy. Members of the house were found to be a part of the Cabal and so the house has lost social standing.

Wilton: A duchy. Members of the house were found to be a part of the Cabal and so the house has lost social standing.

Santir: A duchy. Pellia's House.

Strand: A dead house. A duchy. After revealing Lord Antony Strand's involvement in the Cabal and his subsequent possession, the authorities declared the Strand name extinct. They also transferred all their lands, holdings, and offices back to the crown.

Zaimar: A countdom.

Bellmar: A countdom. Members of the house were found to be a part of the Cabal and so the house has lost social standing.

Orden: A countdom. Zera's House.

Fristly: A countdom.

ABOUT THE AUTHOR

Jordyn Alexander

 Jordyn Alexander has loved fantasy since she was a child and first read The Wizard of Oz. She is incredibly blessed to be able to write what she loves abd live in fantasy worlds during her working hours. Jordyn is a Texas native livingin beautiful San Antonio. She lives with her husband and cats.

The War Brides of Adrik is her first published series.

BOOKS IN THIS SERIES

The War Brides of Adrik
The Kingdom of Arik started a war against the orc Kingdom of Orik. They lost. In a desperate bid to stop the war before there is more slaughter, Queen Adalind of Adrik offers the orcs the only thing they could want that they cannot take with force of arm: willing brides. Starting with Adalind's story, the War Brides of Adrik series takes readers through the passion and romance of these brides as they overcome obstacles and find their happy ends with their orcs.

War Queen

Cursed at birth with fairy-like beauty, Queen Adalind has only ever known pain and death at the hands of men.

Always a prize to be coveted, she doesn't know that she can trust any male. When Adalind must save her kingdom after the death of her cruel husband during a war he started with the nearby orc kingdom, the jaded queen offers herself up as a sacrifice. The orc king will receive a bride with magical beauty and she will save her subjects from more slaughter. What she doesn't expect is to be attracted to her future husband or find him to an honorable orc.

King Rognar is merely seeking to end the war started by the humans, take his pound of flesh and go home.

What he is not expecting is to be challenged by a beautiful, politically savvy queen, who seems to offer him everything he could ever want. But as he gets to see the real woman beneath her icy exterior, he finds that what he truly wants is Adalind's heart. As passion ignites between them, can they trust each other and rule two kingdoms?

Or will all the forces that conspire against them tear them and their kingdoms, apart?

War Mistress

Pellia Santir has always had her choices taken from her, since she was a child.

Finally free from the abusive king she was forced to serve as mistress, Pellia is looking for a fresh start. A new path. And a new lover. When she is installed as Regent of Adrik alongside the quiet and brooding Verrick, she believes she has found that lover. If only she can convince him of that fact.

Verrick ka Roknir is an orc who has been burned by human women before.

Haunted by the memory of a treacherous past-mate, Verrick is determined to never be blinded by beauty again. Even if the flirtatious human regent is oh, so tempting. He resolves for his heart to be as stone, but the pretty human has a way of getting behind his defenses.

When fires break out in the south of the country, caused by an insidious force, Pellia and Verrick are put to the test.

Can they come together to save the country from those that threaten it and ignite the passion growing between them? Or will the enemy destroy them and the land they swore to protect?

War Maiden (Coming Soon)

Dura ka Woreki has always been a shieldmaiden of valor and duty.

Fighting alongside her cousin, King Rognar, she can't imagine that she would ever have to pick between honor and personal feeling. Until, in the heat of battle, her Mating Instinct awakens for an enemy soldier she has sworn to kill. When she makes a split-second decision that she can't take back, Dura saves the soldier and spirits him off into woods where they can hide, abandoning her allegiance for the first time.

Marvik Grimble has only one person in the world that he cares about: his sister Queen Adalind.

Forced by a magical oath to protect her abuser, the twisted King Yorian, Marvik finds himself in the middle of a war that he knows he can't win. When he is gravely injured in battle, he accepts his death, only to find himself saved by the very one that wounded him in the first place. At first, all he wants is to escape, but as he gets to know the brave and feisty Dura, he is no longer sure what he wants.

Both know that they can never go back home, but as they slowly fall for one another, they discover a danger that could rock the foundations of Adrik and Orik.

Can they warn the people they love and find a way to be together or will the duty they've both always carried bring their doom?

Made in the USA
Monee, IL
05 April 2024

56407739R00135